The director clapped his hands. "Let's try that scene again, from the top." The cast got up and moved to their positions.

Sally turned and peered into the darkened side of the stage. "Could I have some more light? It's a little difficult to see right now."

"The light cue's set up for Jaqueline's entrance when she turns on the lamp," the man with the headset replied. "We'd have to reset."

"Oh, for God's sake!" Jaqueline Cantwell threw up her hands. "It's a working lamp, isn't it? Then turn on the lamp!" she barked.

The maid hurriedly set her tea tray down on the sideboard, then reached for the switch on the lamp.

There was a blinding flash of light, followed by a loud explosion. Sally flew backward into the French doors and fell in a crumpled heap on the floor.

This time the screams in the audience were real.

Titles available in the HART AND SOUL series, published by Bantam Books:

HART AND SOUL 2

PLAY DEAD

JAHNNA N. MALCOLM

BANTAM BOOKS
NEW YORK · TORONTO · LONDON · SYDNEY · AUCKLAND

PLAY DEAD

A BANTAM BOOK 0 553 17622 6

First published in USA by Bantam Books, a division of Bantam
Doubleday Dell Publishing Group, Inc.

First publication in Great Britain

PRINTING HISTORY
Bantam edition published 1991

Bantam Books are published by Transworld Publishers Ltd.,
61–63 Uxbridge Road, Ealing, London W5 5SA,
in Australia by Transworld Publishers (Australia) Pty. Ltd.,
15–23 Helles Avenue, Moorebank, NSW 2170, and in New
Zealand by Transworld Publishers (N.Z.) Ltd., Cnr. Moselle
and Waipareira Avenues, Henderson, Auckland.

Made and printed in Great Britain by
BPCC Hazell Books
Aylesbury, Bucks, England
Member of BPCC Ltd.

To our many friends
who have died a thousand deaths on the stage.

With special thanks to
the North Carolina Theatre's cast of *1776*.

CHAPTER ONE

Colonel? Are you ill?"

The officer turned around and staggered toward the young girl. A dagger protruded from his chest, its hilt red with blood. She leaped away in horror. He sprawled forward across the sofa.

A man in an overcoat burst through the French doors and gasped, "How could you!"

"Don't come near me," the young woman hissed. She lunged for the silver pistol on the desk.

There was a blinding flash of lightning, and the casement window above the library stairs burst open. An eerie apparition stood framed in the sill. Fog swirled around its feet. The ghost pointed at the young woman and moaned, "Eloise, you must pay for your sins."

Then a shot rang out, thunder crashed, and a woman in the audience screamed.

Amanda Hart giggled nervously. Watching a dress rehearsal of a professional play was an entirely new experience for her. *Murder at Midnight* was the most talked-about production to open in San Francisco in years. Amanda felt privileged to have been one of the lucky few invited to attend the rehearsal at the Gateway Theatre.

Of course it helped that one of her friends from Sutter Academy was playing the role of the ingenue. As editor of the school newspaper, Amanda knew that a behind-the-scenes story would make a perfect feature for the next issue.

Her friend, Kitty Butterfield, placed the pistol on the table and turned to face the audience. A large tear rolled down her cheek. Amanda leaned forward to catch the actress's words.

Suddenly from out of the dark a voice shouted, "Hold, please!" As the lights came up in the audience, a man in the front row stood up and stepped onto the stage. He was joined by a short, stocky girl, who shouted, "Cast and crew, onstage."

"Why are they stopping?" the redheaded girl sitting beside Amanda whispered. "Things were just getting good."

Amanda smiled at her best friend, Pepper Larson, and shook her head. "I don't know, but let's take advantage of the break."

Amanda stood up and stretched her arms out to the side. Then she smoothed her long red-and-green plaid wool skirt. It was the first chance she'd had to wear it that winter. Her white silk blouse and forest-green vest gave her the look of an old-fashioned schoolgirl. Amanda had added a prim black tie, completing the image. She shook her thick dark hair and then sat back in her seat. "Kitty's doing great, isn't she?"

"I'm definitely impressed." Pepper shoved her wire-rimmed glasses up on her nose. "Especially when she cries. I could only do that if I poked myself in the eye, or sniffed an onion."

"They say if you concentrate on something that made you cry once, you'll do it again. Kitty told me that actors call it sense memory."

Pepper shrugged. "I can think of a lot of sad things, but I'm not sure they would make tears run down my face."

Amanda focused her big green eyes on her friend. "I cry at everything—books, old movies. I can even get emotional over a commercial."

Pepper leaned back in her seat. "I guess I'd have to think of my dog when he got really sick and almost died. Or *Bambi* when his mother was killed. That always chokes me up. Of course, there's the time I dropped my camera in the bay. That *really* made me cry."

Amanda giggled. "By the time you thought of something sad, the play would be over."

"Exactly." Pepper nodded, and her short red hair bounced with each brisk movement. "Which is why I'm in the audience and Kitty's up on stage."

"Ladies and gentlemen?"

The man who'd interrupted the show was speaking to the audience. He tucked a clipboard under his arm and smiled out at the vast auditorium. "Sorry to stop the show, but we're having technical problems with the apparition. It has to be absolutely right for our opening tomorrow night, so just bare with us."

He spoke with the confident tone of someone who is used to being obeyed without question. He was dressed casually in a boatneck sweater, faded Levi's, and worn topsiders. A pair of glasses was pushed up on top of his head. In fact, with his deeply tanned face and unruly blond hair, he looked as if he'd just stepped off a sailboat.

Amanda consulted her program. "I think that's Cliff Verdery, the director."

"Oh!" Pepper nodded. "I've heard of him. Didn't he direct that musical *Razzle Dazzle*?"

"Yeah," Amanda said, "it's been running for three years. He's known as a real whiz. He has two shows running in Chicago, and the rumor is they're planning to move this play to Broadway."

"Broadway!" Pepper's brown eyes widened. "Kitty must be ecstatic."

"Paralyzed with fear is more like it," Amanda said, glancing up at the stage. "Ever since she was cast in this play, she hasn't been the same. I think she eats, drinks, and sleeps the part."

Pepper shrugged. "I wouldn't know. I haven't seen her at school for a whole month."

"Miss Wilson let her out of school as part of a special work-for-credit program."

"It makes sense," Pepper said. "The only thing Kitty wants to do in life is be an actress."

"This is a golden opportunity for her," Amanda declared. "I understand agents from New York and L.A. are going to be here for the opening."

Pepper cocked her head and looked at Amanda. "How do you know all that?"

"A good reporter always does her research." She held up her leatherbound notebook. "I figured if I was going to do an article about Kitty as an actress, I should find out a little more about the play and the people she's working with." Amanda grinned. "Besides, Aunt Jane's on the Council for the Arts and gets the inside scoop."

Amanda was living with her aunt and uncle Pickering while her parents were off on assignment in the Middle East. She missed them terribly, but she understood that their work as photojournalists often took them to places where she couldn't go. Amanda dreamed of following in their footsteps.

"It's really interesting," she said, consulting her notes. "Most of the people on that stage are pretty famous."

"Like who?" Pepper leaned forward and rested her elbows on the seat in front of her.

Amanda pointed to the man in the trench coat. "That's Richard Tyson, the TV star."

"Really?" Pepper sat up. "I used to watch *K. J. Whapper, M.D.* every Wednesday night." She stared at the man with a new intensity. "Boy, he sure has gotten older, hasn't he? Look at those gray streaks in his hair."

Amanda pointed to the "apparition," which was actually a woman dressed in white. "Of course, everyone knows Jaqueline Cantwell. She's not only the star but one of the producers."

"She and her husband, George, did all of those old plays together."

Amanda nodded. "This play was written for her years ago."

"Then how come we've never heard of it?"

"That's the interesting part." Amanda flipped open her notebook and pulled out an article from a recent edition of the *San Francisco Chronicle*. "Her husband died of a heart attack on opening night."

"On the stage?" Pepper sat up straight.

"That's right. The play was canceled, and Jaqueline Cantwell refused to act again."

"Why?"

Amanda consulted the article again. "She said—'Life in the theater was meaningless without her husband.'"

"Wow." Pepper sighed. "That's true love."

"Maybe." Amanda flipped through the pages of her notebook. "I found another article that said no one else would work with her. Kitty says she's the meanest person on earth."

"I've had it with our little ingenue!" Jaqueline Cantwell's voice soared out above them and carried clearly to the back row of the theater.

"Come now, Jaqueline, be reasonable," the director

replied, an impatient edge in his voice. "It's not Kitty's fault that you're late for your entrance. If you'd practiced the quick change with your dresser—as I have *repeatedly* asked you to—there wouldn't be a problem."

"Don't lecture me, young man!" The actress stood up and struck a dramatic pose. "I have graced the stage for more years than you have crawled upon this earth."

"And it shows," a voice muttered from the center aisle. "What a hag!"

Amanda saw that the voice belonged to the stocky blond girl who'd called the cast and crew together onstage. Amanda guessed that the girl must be the stage manager. She was consulting with a man wearing a headset.

"Kitty?" The director waved for Amanda's friend, who was standing meekly at the edge of the stage by the big velvet curtain. "Miss Cantwell feels that you're entering a bit early, babe."

"Early!" Jaqueline Cantwell laughed sarcastically. "Cliff, my love, the girl is deliberately upstaging me."

"Upstaging?" Pepper repeated, mystified.

Amanda, who had taken several drama classes, whispered, "That's a theatrical term for pulling the focus away from the person who's supposed to have it. It means that Miss Cantwell wants to have a big moment when she appears as the ghost, and Kitty's ruining it for her."

"But what does upstage have to do with it?"

"See how the floor is tilted?"

Amanda pointed to the stage, which had been raised at an angle. "Well, the front part is called downstage, because it's the lowest, and the highest part is upstage."

"I get it," Pepper murmured. "So, if you were downstage doing a dramatic speech, and I was behind you making faces—"

"You'd be upstaging me," Amanda finished for her. "And that is a serious crime in the theater." She grinned and added, "Especially if the person you're upstaging is the star."

The two girls looked back at their friend on the stage, who stood accused of the awful crime.

"I'm sorry, Miss Cantwell," Kitty said in a quiet voice. "I had no intention of hurting your performance."

"Oh, spare me!" Miss Cantwell rolled her eyes, then tapped the white-haired actor who'd been playing Colonel Pinchmore on the shoulder. "Teddy dear, get me a cigarette, will you? I need one desperately."

"Certainly, Jaqui." The man rose to his feet with the knife still sticking out of his jacket. He unhooked it from a strap fastened around his chest and set it on the table. Then he disappeared into the wings and quickly returned with a pack of cigarettes and a lighter. Jaqueline Cantwell took them from him without a word of thanks.

"That's Teddy Ballard," Amanda whispered to Pepper. "He's been in a ton of plays."

Pepper squinted up at him. "He looks familiar."

"Oh, you've seen him a thousand times. He plays a

lot of supporting parts in movies. And commercials, too."

"Like what?"

"He's the old butler in that *Nuts-So-Fine* cereal commercial."

"And another thing," Jaqueline announced, lighting her cigarette and blowing the smoke toward the director, "would you please ask Mr. Tyson to look at me when I'm speaking, not at the audience?"

Cliff Verdery put his hands on his hips and faced Jaqueline Cantwell. "I believe there's only one director in this theater."

Jaqueline completely ignored his remark and continued, "And another thing—if that girl playing the maid doesn't learn her cue, I'm having her fired." The actress leaned forward on the couch and asked, "Do you understand me?"

"I'm reading you loud and clear," Cliff Verdery said through clenched teeth.

Pepper whistled low. "It's really weird that they're saying all of this in front of an audience."

Amanda nodded in amazement. "I think they've forgotten we're here." Amanda looked over her shoulder. "I bet there are only fifty people in this entire theater."

Pepper leaned closer and whispered, "It's kind of fun to hear the real dirt."

The two girls giggled conspiratorially and then faced the stage.

"Sally," the director called toward the wings, "let's

go over that tea scene quickly before we continue with rehearsal."

A pretty, dark-haired girl stuck her head out from the side of the stage and said meekly, "I'm ready, Mr. Verdery."

"Good." The director clapped his hands. "Then let's try that scene again, from the top." The cast got up and moved to their positions.

"Everyone in places?" the director shouted. "Let's go."

The door to the library opened, and the dark-haired girl dressed in a maid's uniform entered the room, gingerly carrying a tray filled with cups and saucers. She set the tray on the table with a loud thunk and started to exit.

"No, no, no!" Cliff Verdery bellowed from out in the audience.

"My line!" the girl gasped. "I'm so sorry."

"Sally, what is the problem here?" the director demanded, leaping up on the stage. "You just walk in, put down the tray, say, 'Here is your tea, Miss,' and then go stand by the sideboard." He glanced down at the tray and exclaimed, "Where are the spoons?"

Sally spoke up in a tired voice, "Mr. Verdery, I can't seem to find them."

"They're up there, Sal," the stage manager called from the center aisle. "I set them on the sideboard for you myself."

Sally turned and peered in the darkened side of the stage. "Could I have some more light? It's a little difficult to see right now."

"The light cue's set up for Jaqueline's entrance when she turns on the lamp," the man with the headset replied. "We'd have to reset."

"Oh, for God's sake!" Jaqueline Cantwell threw up her hands. "It's a working lamp, isn't it?"

"Right," the stage manager replied.

"Then turn on the lamp!" Miss Cantwell barked.

The maid hurriedly set her tea tray down on the sideboard, nearly dropping it on the floor.

"Look out!" Teddy shouted.

She quickly righted the tray, then reached for the switch on the lamp.

There was a blinding flash of light, followed by a loud explosion. Sally flew backward into the French doors and fell in a crumpled heap on the floor.

This time the screams in the audience were for real.

CHAPTER TWO

T he ambulance arrived within ten minutes, and the number of people in the Gateway Theatre seemed to double. Reporters, public officials, and anxious staff members milled about in the aisles, talking in hushed tones.

Sally Quince was lying on the couch. A rescue worker knelt beside her, taking her pulse. The actress seemed dazed but otherwise unhurt.

Amanda went to join Kitty while Pepper moved through the crowd, photographing the scene of the accident. As her school newspaper's photographer, she always had her camera at the ready.

"This isn't a good place to talk," Kitty said, pointing to the newspaper reporters who were interviewing everyone. "Let's go upstairs."

Amanda followed Kitty up the aisle to the lobby and then up a set of stairs to the first balcony. Kitty, who was still in costume and makeup, collapsed gratefully into one of the seats by the railing. "I like it up here. I feel much better when I can see everybody."

"Did they find out what happened with the lamp?" Amanda asked, as she sat down on the stairs beside her friend.

Kitty nodded her head. "I talked to Dan Carnegie, the man in charge of the props for this show, and he said the plug on the lamp had been changed."

"What does that do?" Amanda asked, instinctively digging in her pack for her notebook and pen.

"I think it sends a different kind of current into the outlet." Kitty nervously twirled her blond hair around one finger. "I heard him say something about running two-twenty voltage through a one-ten line."

Amanda made a note to talk to her cousin, Josh, who knew all about electricity. "Does Dan think the switch was deliberate?"

"I'm not sure, but Skitch is furious about it. She thinks Dan changed the plug himself, and forgot about it because he's so old."

Amanda was writing everyone's name in a column on one side of the page and identifying their jobs in a second column. "Who is Skitch?"

Kitty leaned forward and pointed at the stage. "She's our stage manager. That's her down there, talking to the medics. Short blond hair, chinos, kind of heavy-set."

Amanda peered over the railing to the floor below.

Skitch held a clipboard under one arm, and every few seconds she'd bark an order at the crew, who were trying to keep curious audience members off the stage.

A familiar face bobbing through the crowd beneath them caught Amanda's attention. In her tie-dyed red-and-yellow shirt and stockings that stuck out from under her jean jumper, she was hard to miss.

"Pepper!" Amanda called from the balcony. "Up here."

Pepper pushed her glasses up her nose and squinted in the direction of Amanda's voice. Then she waved and jogged up the center aisle of the theatre.

Moments later, Pepper joined them in the balcony, a little out of breath. "Boy, I'd hate to be an usher in this place. It's like climbing straight up. You'd need an oxygen tank to get to the second balcony."

For the first time since the accident Kitty smiled. "It's pretty steep, isn't it? But it brings the audience closer to the stage."

Pepper inched cautiously toward the railing. "If you tripped and fell off this balcony, you'd land right in that medic's lap."

"Is Sally okay?" Kitty asked.

Pepper nodded. "She's suffering a mild case of shock, but the paramedics say she's going to be okay. They're taking her to the hospital for observation, though, just in case."

On the floor below, they watched the medics lift Sally onto a waiting stretcher, then carry her down from the stage.

"Poor Sally," Kitty said. "She was nervous enough as it was."

Amanda nodded. "I noticed that. She could barely set her tea tray on the table. Why?"

"A lot of weird things have been happening in rehearsal. Sally, who's really superstitious, is sure that the show is cursed."

"Wait a minute," Amanda said, leaning forward. "What kinds of things?"

"Some of them were ridiculous. Like the first time we used the tea set, one of the cups of tea had bleach in it."

"I hope no one drank it," Pepper said.

"Luckily, Miss Cantwell discovered it." Kitty shrugged. "But that was just an accident. The prop assistant was cleaning things and forgot to empty that cup. He was fired."

"I can see why," Pepper murmured.

"Anything else?" Amanda asked, flipping to another page in her notebook.

Kitty nodded and chewed on one fingernail. "When we moved from the rehearsal hall to this theatre, everything started to go wrong. A sandbag dropped and nearly hit several of us. Then the trapdoor in the center of the stage was left open. Richard Tyson almost fell into it. He could have broken his leg."

"Or worse," Amanda said, pursing her lips.

"And now this thing with the lamp." Kitty sighed heavily. "It's almost as if someone were deliberately trying to sabotage the show."

"Maybe someone is." Amanda studied Kitty's face.

Fear was definitely in her eyes. "How well do you know the cast?"

"Not well at all," Kitty said. "I mean, we talk in rehearsal, but that's it. They're all a lot older than me."

"How about the crew?"

"I've only really met Dan Carnegie, but he seems like a nice man." She gestured toward the stage. "That's him, holding the lamp."

Amanda and Pepper peered over the railing at a tall, thin man in coveralls. His hair was gray, and he had the telltale slump that came with age. Amanda guessed he was probably in his late sixties. He kept looking at the lamp and shaking his head.

Amanda folded her arms across her lap. "I guess the question is, who would want to keep this play from opening?"

Kitty shook her head. "No one. This play is very important to all of us. I mean, it could go to Broadway."

Pepper stuck her head between them. "Maybe it's someone from another theatre."

"Do you think so?" Kitty asked.

"It's a possibility," Amanda said, tucking her hair behind one ear. "But there's also the chance that all of these accidents have been aimed at one person." She referred to her notebook. "How well do you know the girl who got shocked?"

"Sally? Not very well."

"Think someone might have it in for her?"

"I don't see why. Besides, Sally never touches that lamp during the play," Kitty replied. "Only Jaqueline

and I ever turn it on. It was sheer luck that we stopped
the scene there and Sally happened to turn it on. It
could just as easily have been me." Kitty shivered at
the thought.

"Maybe you should quit," Pepper said quietly.

"The play?" Kitty's blue eyes widened.

"Of course," Pepper replied. "If your life's in danger—"

"I didn't say that," Kitty said quickly. "Besides, I
could never quit. I have agents coming up from Hollywood. This is my big break."

Pepper shrugged. "What's the use of a big break if
you're not around to enjoy it?"

"Oh, Pepper, you're exaggerating!"

Amanda spoke up. "I agree with Pepper. If this is as
serious as it sounds, you could get hurt."

"When's opening night?" Pepper asked.

"Tomorrow." Kitty clutched Amanda's hand. "I wish
there were some way you could stay with me at least
through the opening. I know you'd be able to figure
this out."

"Me?" Amanda shook her head. "I'm not a detective. I'm just a high school reporter."

"When someone was trying to keep the paper at
Sutter from being published, you found out who was
behind it and risked your life doing it."

"Yeah, I'd say that uncovering a shoplifting ring
qualifies you as a detective," Pepper added.

"You helped solve that case, too, Pepper."

"I know." Pepper grinned. "But you were the brains
behind the whole operation."

"That was a onetime thing, and it was at our school," Amanda countered. "This involves the theatre, something I know very little about."

At that moment they heard deep voices sounding from further up in the balcony behind them. The girls turned to see Cliff Verdery, the director, talking to a short, balding man with glasses.

"Sally is in shock," the director said. "She was a mass of nerves before this and couldn't remember one line. Imagine what she'll be like on opening."

"It just doesn't seem fair to fire her," the balding man said.

"Look, Alfred, do you want your play to be a success, or not?" the director demanded.

"Well, of course," the playwright answered.

"Then write the part out."

"Why can't we just recast the role? It seems much simpler."

"When?" The director threw up his hands. "I don't have a spare minute. I have to deal with publicity, work with the technical department, hold rehearsal, and fight with that awful woman."

There was silence as the playwright mulled over the director's words. Kitty, who had been sitting very still, suddenly stood up. "Excuse me, Mr. Verdery, I don't mean to eavesdrop, but I think I may have a solution to your problem."

"What is it?" The director sounded irritated.

"Well, my friend Amanda Hart just watched the rehearsal. She's done lots of plays, and she and Sally are exactly the same size."

"Get to the point, Kitty."

"Amanda could play the maid. You wouldn't have to refit her costume, or anything."

"What!" Amanda couldn't believe her ears. She had never stepped foot on the stage, let alone in a professional production. It made her heart race just thinking about the thousands of people in the audience. She stood up and moved quickly to join her friend. "Now, wait a min—"

Kitty cut her off. "Mr. Verdery, this is Amanda Hart."

The director didn't respond to the introduction. He just stared hard at Amanda. "Can you talk?"

"And walk," Amanda replied, feeling highly insulted. "And both at the same time."

The director raised an eyebrow at her forwardness. "It just might work," he spoke over his shoulder to the playwright. "The part really isn't difficult, she just enters—"

"Puts the tray on the table, and says, 'Here is your tea, miss,'" Amanda finished. The director raised both eyebrows this time, obviously impressed. "I watched the rehearsal," Amanda explained.

"Okay, we'll go with you," the director said, sticking out his hand. "What's your name again?"

"Amanda Hart." She shook his hand firmly. "But—"

"Work out the details with Skitch," he cut in.

"But—"

"Now this is only to get us through opening," he added brusquely. "After that we may have to recast with a professional. We'll just play it by ear."

"But—"

"Your contract, yes, I know, Skitch will have one for you to sign before rehearsal tomorrow," he replied. "Which, by the way, starts *promptly* at noon."

Before she could say another word, he grabbed the playwright by the arm. "Listen, Alfred, I've been thinking. Can't you come up with a better curtain line for Act One? What we've got isn't working at all."

The girls stared in mute amazement as he pulled the smaller man off into a dimly lit corner of the theatre.

"Tomorrow morning?" Amanda finally spoke. "But I don't want to be in a play. That's the *last* thing I want to do. Besides, I have school tomorrow."

"Miss Wilson will let you out. It's only for one day, and after that we work only at night." Kitty hugged her tight. "Oh, Mandy, this is wonderful. You've got the perfect cover for your investigation."

"What investigation?" Amanda protested.

Kitty paid no attention. "Come on downstairs and I'll have you meet Skitch." She led a stunned Amanda back down the stairs toward the stage door, babbling away merrily. "Oh, this will be great fun. Lots of casting agents will be here. You're really pretty; I'm sure they'll love you. Maybe you could get a modeling contract. You're tall enough."

"I don't *want* a modeling contract," Amanda said, pulling her arm away.

Kitty stopped and blinked her big, blue eyes at Amanda. "But, Mandy, I thought you wanted to help me."

"You know, it would make a neat article for the *Spectator*," Pepper said. "The inside scoop on theatre life, from someone who's never acted before."

"If it's so interesting," Amanda snapped at Pepper, "why don't you volunteer?"

Pepper shoved her glasses up on her nose and looked directly into Amanda's green eyes. "Because my place is behind the camera. I take pictures. You, on the other hand, are a writer. I don't think you've considered the possibilities for an article like this."

"What possibilities?"

"There are magazines—like *Seventeen*, *Sassy*, *Cosmo*—that would probably be interested in a story like this. Isn't that how your parents got started?"

"In a play?"

"No, out there covering stories they weren't sure of."

"Pepper, my parents cover wars and—and famines. *Important* things."

"Theatre is important!" Kitty said indignantly.

"I know it is," Amanda said, "it's just that . . ." Her voice trailed off uncertainly.

"What?" Pepper demanded.

"Well . . . I'm afraid."

"Of the audience?" Kitty asked.

"Not that. Haven't we forgotten something important here?" She put her hands on her hips and stared sternly at her friends. "Just moments ago, Sally Quince was nearly electrocuted. What if more of these so-called accidents happen? I don't want to leave this place on a stretcher. I prefer walking, thank you very much!"

Kitty took a deep breath. "I have a strong feeling that if we can just get through the opening tomorrow night, everything will be all right."

Amanda looked unconvinced.

"Mandy, it's a lot to ask, I know," Kitty said quietly. "But I'd feel a hundred times better knowing you were going to be with me in this play. We could watch out for each other."

"Sure you won't quit?" Amanda asked.

Kitty smiled weakly. "I can't. It means too much to my career." She placed her hand gently on Amanda's shoulder. "Don't say anything right now. I've got to go change. I'll meet you outside in a few minutes, and you can tell me what you've decided then." She turned and walked down the aisle toward the stage.

Amanda followed Pepper out through the lobby, and the two girls stood outside the stage door in silence. Then Amanda looked up to find Pepper eyeing her with amusement. "What are you grinning at?" she demanded.

"You," Pepper replied. "I can tell you're dying to figure out who's trying to sabotage the show."

"It is intriguing," Amanda admitted. "But I don't know. There's the danger involved."

"Sure, I understand," Pepper said. "You could leave Kitty on her own. After all, it's not your problem."

"Then again, it's only for a day or two."

"And just to be on the safe side," Pepper said, a twinkle in her eye, "we could hire a bodyguard."

Amanda's heart skipped a beat. "You mean . . . ?"

Pepper nodded vigorously. "Dial FLEET ST."

Fleet Street was a bicycle messenger service Amanda had called when her articles about school sororities led to anonymous threats against her life. Amanda closed her eyes briefly, thinking of the boy who had answered her call, and a succession of images flooded through her mind. Blue eyes sparkling with humor. The unruly shock of black hair. A worn leather jacket with the collar turned up against the fog. The flash of his bicycle spokes in the sun.

He'd saved her life during the sorority case, then disappeared without another word.

Amanda bit her lip, thinking. "He's probably forgotten all about us. Besides, he wouldn't be interested."

"You never know," a husky voice replied. "Why don't you give him a try?"

CHAPTER THREE

Mickey Soul leaned casually against the brick wall of the theatre, his arms folded across his chest. The collar of his worn leather jacket was turned up against the late evening chill. His faded jeans fit him like a second skin. His mirrored aviator sunglasses reflected the neon lights of the street above his smooth, lean chin. With a quick movement he reached up and took them off. The dark shock of hair that fell over one eye identified him like a signature.

Amanda turned to Pepper, then back to Mick, and then back to Pepper, unable to utter a word.

"It's Mick," Pepper prompted. "Remember?"

"Of course I remember."

His lips curled into the familiar half-smile as he

watched Amanda's face. "Pepper told me that you'd be here tonight, so I figured I'd join you."

"Pepper?"

Her friend was suddenly preoccupied with examining the lens cap of her Nikon.

"Pepper!" Amanda repeated more firmly.

"Hmm?"

"You didn't tell me you'd talked to Mick."

Pepper raised her head and blinked her brown eyes innocently. "Didn't I?"

Amanda shot silent daggers with her eyes.

"Oh!" Pepper hit herself in the head. "I remember. I thought it'd be a surprise."

"Well, it certainly is."

Amanda hadn't seen or heard from Mick in almost a month. At first, she had checked the mail daily, hoping for some word from him. She had even monitored her aunt and uncle's answering machine on the off chance he might phone.

Now here he was and she felt furious. "Long time no see." She bit off her words icily.

"Yeah. Too long." His frankly admiring smile was as unnerving as it was charming. "You're looking good."

She put her hands on her hips. "What did you do, break your hand?"

"What do you mean?" His blue eyes met hers steadily.

"I waited for you to call."

"You waited?" Mick cocked an eyebrow and grinned.

"Don't flatter yourself," Amanda retorted. "I didn't wait that long."

"Hey, chill out," Mick said. "I did call you."

"You did?" Amanda was totally taken aback.

"Several times, but you weren't home." He crossed his arms. "You're *never* home."

"Well, I didn't get the message." She squinted suspiciously at him. "Who did you talk to?"

"Josh." Mick shrugged. "I told him that I'd try later."

"Josh?" Amanda shouted. Her cousin hadn't said a word to her about it. "What is this, a conspiracy?"

She glared at Pepper, who smiled back pleasantly.

"And while we're on the subject of broken hands," Mick said sarcastically, "my phone hasn't been ringing off the hook."

"I've been busy." Amanda shrugged. "Dating, and all that."

"Dating?" Mick dropped his arms to his sides. "Who? That dimwit Elliot?"

Brad Elliot was president of the Student Council at Sutter Academy and was always trying to put the make on Amanda.

"Maybe," Amanda replied. "And he's not a dimwit. He's a little stiff, but he's not stupid." Amanda couldn't believe herself. She couldn't stand Brad Elliot, and here she was, defending him.

"Ha!" Mick chortled. "Face it, the guy's a geek."

"You should know!" Amanda shot back.

Pepper snorted with laughter, and they both turned on her furiously.

"What are you laughing at?" Amanda snap

"Yeah, what's so funny?" Mick demanded.

"You two." She checked her watch and burst out laughing again. "Less than a minute together and you guys are already fighting." Pepper folded her arms and beamed triumphantly. "That's the Hart and Soul I remember."

"Fighting?" Mick and Amanda repeated. "Us?" They looked at each other and burst out laughing. "Never."

"Well, now that you two are talking again," Pepper shouted over their merriment, "maybe we can discuss Mandy's need for a bodyguard."

"What?" Mick stopped laughing.

"Just a minute, Pepper!" Amanda protested, but Pepper ignored her.

"You see, our friend Kitty is in the play, and things are getting *très* weird at this theatre. I'm talking not-so-random accidents, people nearly dying. You get the picture?"

Mick nodded.

"So . . ." Pepper took a deep breath. "Our friend Kitty got Amanda cast in the play as a cover to find out who's the scumbag behind all of the accidents. Now Mandy needs someone to watch over her while she noses around." Pepper looked at Mick. "Get it?"

"Got it."

"Good."

"Hold it right there." Amanda stepped between Pepper and Mick. "Look, I haven't really decided if I'm going to do this play."

"Amanda Hart?" a voice asked from behind her. "I'm Skitch Hall, *Murder*'s stage manager. Rehearsal begins at noon, but we need you here by eleven for a costume fitting. Don't be late. Cliff, the director, hates people to be late." She started to leave and then turned back. "And so do I."

"Don't I get a script, or something?"

The girl made a brief note on her clipboard. "I'll have one for you in the green room at eleven. With your contract."

"Green room," Amanda repeated.

"Yeah, it's beneath the stage between the dressing rooms," Skitch said. "The actors' lounge." Then, for the first time in the entire conversation, the girl smiled. "Welcome aboard, Amanda."

Skitch disappeared back into the theatre.

"What were you saying about not having made up your mind?" Pepper asked slyly.

Amanda shook her head. "These theatre people sure assume a lot. I haven't once said I would do the show."

"I guess they figure everybody wants to be a star," Pepper cracked.

The stage door burst open, and a man and a woman emerged into the alley.

"Don't think you can get away with this, Jaqueline!" the man said angrily. "You can't push me around."

Richard Tyson stood directly under the light atop the stage door, wearing an expensive trench coat. He was still a very handsome man, although the harsh streetlight revealed the lines of age that makeup concealed on the stage. His hair was obviously dyed, with just the right amount of gray left at the temples to give him a distinguished look.

"Oh, really, Richard!" Jaqueline Cantwell wrapped her suede coat with the fox collar around her shoulders. "If you wanted to share top billing, your agent should have negotiated it into your contract."

Richard Tyson pursued the actress down the alley toward the street. "For your information, Miss Cantwell, I had a hit series that ran for four years on prime time." He buttoned his coat as he spoke, punctuating each word with an angry twist of his wrist.

"Hit series!" She lit a cigarette and exhaled on a laugh. "K. J. Flapper?"

"WHAPPER!" he corrected angrily.

"Sorry, darling, you didn't even make it into syndication," Jaqueline cooed. "Besides, that was five years ago. What have you done lately? The only people who will come to see you are those morbid creatures who want to see how cruelly the years have treated you."

"More people saw me in one episode of that show," he shot back, "than ever saw you in all of your theatre productions put together."

"A perfect example of how low standards have fallen in this country." She took a long drag on her cigarette, then lowered her voice to a sympathetic tone. "Richard, dear—face the facts. Since you were canceled, you've had guest spots on a couple of game shows. Do you really think *that* makes you a star?"

From where they stood, Amanda and the others

could see Richard's face turn red with rage. The veins on his forehead stood out, and he looked like he was about to explode. Suddenly he raised his arm, and for one awful second Amanda thought he was going to hit his leading lady. Instead, he grabbed the belt on his trench coat and pulled it tight. He spun on his heel and marched to the street.

"Taxi!" A yellow cab screeched to a stop at the curb. Richard opened the door and tossed his bag into the backseat. "I can't believe it!" he muttered to the driver. "Miss Can't-Act-Well calling *me* a has-been. At least George had a glimmer of talent. After he died, she was *forced* to retire. No one would go near her with a ten-foot pole. And she calls *me* washed up!"

He watched Jaqueline Cantwell disappear through the door of a restaurant across the street, and a look of pure hatred disfigured his matinee idol features. "Wait here," he barked at the driver. "I'll be right back."

"Man, is he tweaked," Mick said as they watched the actor cross the street to the restaurant. "I wouldn't want to get in his way right now."

Pepper shook her head sadly. "*K. J. Whapper* was one of my favorite shows in sixth grade. He was so cool. Now he's just old."

"Mandy!" Kitty Butterfield called from the stage door. "I just talked to Skitch, and she says you're in! That's wonderful!"

"That your friend?" Mick asked. When Amanda nodded, Mick whistled low under his breath. Kitty was still wearing her dramatic stage makeup, and her blond hair framed her face like a soft cloud. She had on a full-length black coat with a long red scarf, and as she paused under the stage door light, she looked every inch the grand actress she hoped to become.

"You know, I like Kitty," Pepper murmured to Amanda, "but lately it's as if she's always onstage. Look at her standing there—like she's posing for the cover of *Premiere* magazine."

"She must not have had time to take off her stage makeup," Amanda said. "And her hair was fixed like that for the play."

"Who cares how she does it?" Mick said with a grin. "All that matters is that she does it."

Amanda resisted the sudden wave of jealousy that washed over her. Normally she thought of Kitty as one of her closer friends, but at this moment, she wished Kitty would just disappear. Amanda shook her head in dismay. *You haven't seen Mick in almost a month*, she thought, *and all of a sudden you're acting like a jealous girlfriend. Get a grip on yourself!*

"Introduce me," Mick murmured as the actress drew near.

"Kitty," Amanda said, forcing a big smile, "I'd like you to meet a good friend of ours. Mickey Soul, meet Kitty Butterfield."

Mick shook her hand. "My pleasure."

Kitty cocked her head to look at Mick. "You look familiar. Haven't we met before?"

Mick grinned. "That's my line."

Amanda's green eyes suddenly widened as she remembered that they probably *had* met before, when Mick had attended Sutter Academy for a week. He'd disguised himself as her fictional cousin, Michael Soultaire, so that he could keep a close watch on her.

"Mick looks like a lot of people," Amanda replied hurriedly.

"Not the people I know," Kitty murmured. She lowered her chin and gazed up soulfully into his eyes.

When she fluttered her eyelashes, Pepper groaned. "Getting pretty thick around here, isn't it?"

"Let's go, driver!" Richard Tyson barked as he returned to the cab. He saw Kitty, and his expression softened. "Kitty, can I give you a lift home?"

"Why, thank you, Richard!" Kitty flashed a big smile in the actor's direction. "I'd really appreciate it." She turned back to Amanda and whispered, "I'm hoping he'll introduce me to his agent. Talk to you later."

The cab drove off, and suddenly Geary Street looked deserted.

"Guess I'd better get going, too," Amanda said reluctantly. "I've got a lot of things to do before rehearsal tomorrow."

Mick looped one leg over his ten-speed. "Then I'll see you at noon."

"Where?" Amanda asked.

"Inside the theatre." Mick hopped onto the seat and pedaled down the alley toward the street.

"Wait!" Amanda called as he jumped the curb. "Aren't you going to tell me how?"

"And spoil the surprise?" Mick popped a wheelie and sped off, shouting, "Never."

CHAPTER FOUR

The next day Amanda arrived at the stage door of the Gateway Theatre fifteen minutes early. She'd remembered the stage manager's warning about not being late, and she wanted to give herself enough time to find the green room.

Amanda had spent the morning in Miss Wilson's office at Sutter Academy. Surprisingly, the headmistress, who was usually very no-nonsense about things, was thrilled to hear about Amanda's being cast in the production. Miss Wilson had agreed to excuse Amanda from school on two conditions: one, that she use her experience to write several reports for her English and Journalism classes, and two, that she reserve a seat for Miss Wilson on opening night.

"Imagine! Two of our students in a professional

play," the headmistress said, her face beaming with pride. "Quite a coup for the academy."

Of course, Miss Wilson's words only served to make Amanda even more nervous about being onstage. She knew she was going to have to perform in front of an audience, but it had never occurred to her that people she *knew* might be watching.

The metal stage door clanged shut behind her as she stepped into the theatre. Amanda paused for a moment to let her eyes adjust to the gloom of backstage. A heavy-set man in coveralls stepped in front of her. "Need something?"

"I'm Amanda Hart," she replied, her voice sounding timid and small in her ears. "I'm in the play."

The man ran his finger down a list posted by the door. He grunted and said, "Okay." Without looking back at her he settled his imposing bulk into a swivel chair by the door and picked up a newspaper.

"I'm looking for the, uh . . . green room?"

He gestured with his thumb to the far wall. "Go down one floor, cross under the stage, and you'll find the green room."

Amanda did as she was told and stepped gingerly down the stairs. The plaster walls felt slightly damp, and the air smelled old and musty. At the bottom she could see a light glowing at the end of the corridor.

Amanda felt certain something horrible, like a rat, would leap out at her at any moment. She ducked her head and kept her arms close to her sides, trying to hurry as fast as she could.

She passed a small white door that was ajar. Amanda

peeked through it into a dark well that contained chairs and music stands. Looking up, Amanda could see that the stage floor had been extended over the cramped space to cover it up. Faint footsteps could be heard overhead as the stagehands made last-minute adjustments to the set.

"This must be the orchestra pit," she said to the darkness. "Pit is right. Whatever happened to the glamorous world of theatre?"

"It's all an illusion, dear heart, didn't you know that?"

Amanda squealed and threw herself back against the wall. Standing behind her was a portly gentleman with snow-white hair. He carried a leather bag over one shoulder. After a moment she recognized him as Teddy Ballard, the actor who played Colonel Pinchmore.

"You scared me," Amanda gasped. "I didn't know you were there."

"I'm sorry I frightened you," he said sincerely as he continued on his way. "These tunnels are soundproof. People could get trapped down here, scream their lungs out, and no one would hear them."

Amanda shivered and quickened her pace to get to the end of the tunnel. She burst into a room that had two old couches, an ancient Oriental rug, and a battered coffee table in the middle of it. Several middle-aged women stood chatting at one end. They were all wearing identical blue smocks, with pins attached to the sleeves and tape measures draped around their necks.

Skitch Hall, the stage manager, was talking on the wall phone. She spotted them and hung up. "Teddy, I've been trying to reach you all morning. You had a costume fitting at ten-thirty."

"Did I?" the white-haired gentleman replied. He bowed extravagantly toward the ladies in the smocks. "Forgive me, my dears, but it slipped my mind "

Skitch was not charmed. She checked her watch and said, "Richard's in there right now. You and Amanda will just have to be fitted at the same time."

Amanda's eyes widened. She knew theatre people were uninhibited, but she hadn't counted on having to dress with anyone else. Skitch saw her look, and a tiny smile flickered across her lips. "In different rooms, of course."

"Ah, so you are to be our new maid," Teddy Ballard said.

Amanda nodded. "I'm Amanda Hart."

"Unlucky break for poor Sally," he commented as he adjusted the mauve-and-gray scarf loosely knotted around his neck. "The strangest accidents happen in the theatre. Who would ever think acting could be so dangerous?"

"Are you sure it was an accident?" Amanda asked, her reporter's curiosity aroused. "I heard different."

"Not an accident?" Teddy nearly choked. "Where did you hear that?"

Before Amanda could reply, Teddy turned on Skitch. "Why weren't the actors informed of this?"

Skitch shot Amanda an irritated look, then sighed heavily. "Now, Teddy, don't get upset. It's just a rumor.

Personally, I think the lighting crew goofed up and is trying to cover their behind. In the meantime, until we know exactly what happened, the crew is taking extra precautions, okay?"

"That's all very fine for you and the crew to take precautions, but what about us in the cast?" He poked his chest with his finger for emphasis. "*We're* the ones who put our lives on the line every night."

Skitch nodded patiently. "I'll make a company announcement before rehearsal today."

"See that you do!" Teddy snapped. Just as quickly, his attitude softened and he looked like the jovial Colonel Pinchmore that Amanda remembered. "It wouldn't do for our new actress to think we didn't care."

"I suppose not." The stage manager already had her mind on something else. She turned to Amanda, "You'll be in fitting room three in five minutes."

Amanda nodded. As Skitch walked away, Teddy whispered, "The first lesson in theatre is to never let anyone walk over you. All techies think actors are idiots, and it's our job to inform them otherwise."

"What's a techie?" Amanda asked, wishing she'd brought her notebook to write things down.

"My, you *are* new, aren't you." Teddy settled down in the center of the couch and stretched his arms out across the back of the old faded green sofa. "Techies are the folks behind the scenes—lights and sound, sets and props, costumes and wigs, and so on. They'll tell you that a play is nothing without them, but don't believe a word of it."

Teddy's voice deepened dramatically as he spoke.

"All an actor needs is an empty space and an audience to make a play. We are the high priests at the altar of this, the noblest of artistic callings—"

"For Pete's sake, Teddy, give the poor girl a break," Richard Tyson groaned as he emerged from the fitting room. "It's her first day of rehearsal, and you're already boring her with your 'Acting Is Art' lecture."

Teddy didn't seem fazed at all. Instead he asked Amanda, "Are you bored, my dear?"

"Not a bit." Amanda was fascinated. People in the theatre really were larger than life.

"Uh-oh," Richard said, shaking his head as he smiled at her. "You've just sealed your fate. Teddy has now been given permission to talk your ear off."

Richard seemed totally different from the angry man she'd seen the night before. Today he was really charming, much like the TV character he'd played years before.

"Teddy and Amanda?" one of the ladies in the smocks called. "We're ready for you now."

"Coming, love." As Teddy passed Amanda, he whispered, "If they so much as touch you with one of those dreadful straight pins, scream bloody murder." His blue eyes twinkled as he added, "It makes them crazy."

Amanda giggled as she hurried toward the third fitting room. The tiny room consisted of two corkboard walls covered in safety pins, a full-length mirror at one end, and a curtain. Three ladies were already inside. The oldest one of them pulled the black-and-white maid's costume off the rack and handed it to Amanda. "I'm Mrs. Cunningham. I know it feels like you're dressing in a phone booth," she said, "but it's much faster this way."

For the next fifteen minutes Amanda felt like a mannequin. The three ladies bustled about her, totally absorbed in their task. They pulled this and pinned that, all the while talking about Amanda as if she weren't there.

"I think we should shorten it to show off her legs," a plump woman with glasses suggested. "She has nice, long legs."

"Are you kidding?" Mrs. Cunningham replied. "The Dragon Lady'd hit the roof. Miss Cantwell would have our heads on a plate if we let her be upstaged by a pair of legs."

The third lady, who was tall and thin as a rail, giggled. "It'd serve her right. Turn, please." Amanda spun first to the right, then to the left. She lifted her arms and bent her knees on their command, all the time listening to their conversation.

"Look what happened to that poor Sally Quince," the plump woman clucked sympathetically.

Mrs. Cunningham nodded. "Jaqueline couldn't stand her. She had me alter the girl's costume three times."

The plump woman took several pins out of her mouth and said, "You don't think Miss Cantwell had anything to do with that lamp, do you?"

Amanda watched Mrs. Cunningham's guarded reaction in the mirror. "All I'm saying is, Sally was a nervous wreck and Jaqueline is much happier now that she's gone."

The plump woman snickered. "Wait till she sees Sally's replacement. She's going to be madder than ever."

Amanda coughed, and the three ladies stopped talking. Finally Mrs. Cunningham said, "Miss Cantwell can be hard on young girls, but if you keep your mouth shut and stay out of her way, you'll be fine."

"You'll be just fine," the other two echoed.

Amanda didn't feel fine at all. In fact, she was starting to feel a little woozy. She told herself it was from spending half an hour standing stock-still with her arms held out to the side. But another part of her knew better. Could Miss Cantwell have caused Sally's accident for such a petty reason?

"Look here, I need a proper military uniform. I'm a colonel, not a crossing guard at the local elementary school!" Teddy Ballard's voice could be heard bellowing from the next cubicle. "And how do you expect me to bend my arm? I may play a dead man, but you don't have to dress me in a mummy bag."

"Oh, no," Mrs. Cunningham whispered. "It's Teddy. We'd better go calm him down."

The three ladies scurried out, leaving Amanda pinned into her costume. There was no way she could get out of it, and there was no way she could sit down without stabbing herself in several places.

"Pssst! Mandy," a soft voice called from the hallway outside.

"Pepper?" Amanda had never been so relieved to hear her friend's voice. "In here."

Pepper stuck her curly red head through the curtain and grinned. "You look hotter than hot."

"Don't say that in front of Miss Cantwell," Amanda warned. "I understand she likes her maids to look like nuns."

Pepper stepped through the curtain. "This place is a madhouse. Miss Wilson said I could cover the play for extra credit, but when I got here this grumpy guy in overalls stopped me at the stage door."

"He stopped me, too," Amanda said, trying to delicately bend her arm to scratch her head. "How'd you get past him?"

"He asked me if I was working as a dresser, and I said yes." Pepper giggled. "So here I am, ready to be a dresser."

"Oh, Pepper, that's fantastic!" Amanda hugged her friend happily. "I feel much better knowing you're around."

"Ouch!" Pepper squealed as a straight pin jabbed her in the shoulder. "That dress is lethal."

"Well, now that you're a dresser, get me out of this thing." Amanda turned around so her friend could unpin her. "Have you see Kitty?"

Pepper nodded at her in the mirror. "Yeah, she breezed through the lounge area a few minutes ago." Pepper lowered her voice. "I hate to say this, but I think Kitty is overdoing it with the actress routine. She called me 'Pepper, darling.' Can you believe it?"

Amanda nodded emphatically. "I believe it. Everyone around here is like that."

"Hmph!" Pepper stuck the pins back into the wall. "I liked her much better when she was just a regular run-of-the-mill senior at Sutter."

"Me, too," Amanda agreed.

"Places for Act One!" Skitch's voice blared over an intercom speaker in the hall. "Actors onstage for Act One."

"Well, if you like the uniform so much, wear it yourself," Teddy's voice roared. "I have a rehearsal to get to!"

The girls listened to the curtain snap open and his footsteps pound off down the corridor.

"What do you have to do to get decent treatment in this miserable excuse for a theatre?" Richard Tyson's voice boomed from the green room. "My dressing room is still a pigsty! There are no light bulbs, the toilet doesn't work, and it hasn't been cleaned since the last show."

"Has anybody seen my script?" Kitty's plaintive voice could be heard. "I'm sure I left it right here in the green room."

The intercom crackled, and an angry male voice could be heard shouting, "If the entire cast isn't up here in two minutes, I'll fine every one of them!"

Then Skitch's unruffled voice came across the speaker. "Actors, second call, places for Act One."

Pepper shook her head in amazement. "Is everyone in show biz always this uptight? I couldn't take it."

"Me either." Amanda hurriedly threw on her

sweater and jeans. "I just hope I can get through today." As an afterthought she asked, "You haven't seen Mick, have you?"

"Not a sign of him."

"I knew we couldn't depend on him," Amanda grumbled. "He's a flake. A number-one flake. He just walks back into my life and out again, without so much as a 'So long, it's been good to know you.'"

Pepper shrugged. "That's Mick."

The loudspeaker blared. "Onstage. Now!"

Amanda buttoned her jeans and shrieked, "Coming!" Then she calmly turned to Pepper and asked, "How did I ever let myself get talked into this?"

"Just stupid, I guess." Pepper crossed her eyes at her friend.

Amanda stuck out her tongue, then raced down the corridor and up the stairs to rehearsal.

CHAPTER FIVE

Amanda stepped onto the set of *Murder at Midnight* and directly into the middle of an argument between Skitch and the director, Cliff Verdery.

"We agreed to delay rehearsal until noon. Fine. Well, it's noon! Where is she?" The director threw up his arms in exasperation.

"Cliff, when I called Jaqueline's hotel, the clerk said she had already left. She must be on her way." Skitch spoke in a calm voice, but it was obvious that her nerves were starting to get a little frayed. "All we can do is wait."

"Oh, Miss Cantwell would like that! To arrive and have us all just sitting around waiting for her." Cliff gestured to the first few rows of the auditorium, where most of the cast had gathered. "Well, that's not going to happen. Let's get on with this rehearsal. Where's the new girl?"

Amanda, who had tried to back away unobtrusively, spoke up in the tiniest voice. "I'm right here."

"Is that the loudest you can speak?" Cliff barked at her. "Come on, babe, that will never do. See those balconies up there?"

Amanda tilted her head back to take in the two tiers of seats dimly visible high up in the theatre.

"They pay a lot of money for their tickets. If they can't hear you, they're going to be pretty angry."

No one had ever accused Amanda of being shy, but the way everyone was treating her made her want to stick her head in a hole.

"Well?" he demanded impatiently. "Do you understand?"

"I understand perfectly." Her voice rang firmly through the stillness of the auditorium. She made sure to clip her consonants crisply, something she'd learned in speech class.

"Better." The director turned to the stage manager. "Call the actors onstage for Scene Three. Have everyone else sit tight until I need them."

Skitch moved to the control panel sitting behind the curtain off to the right side of the stage. She flipped a switch and spoke into a microphone. "Teddy Ballard, Richard Tyson—onstage, please."

The director turned to Amanda. "Okay, babe, you know what you're supposed to do."

Amanda shook her head. "No, I don't."

"Didn't Skitch give you a script?"

Amanda shook her head. "She promised to give me one today."

The explosion was immediate. "What-is-*wrong*-with-everybody?" he shouted up into the rafters, running all his words together as if they were one long word. "Do you even know the plot?"

"I know it up until the apparition appears," Amanda replied. "Then I'm not sure what happens. That's where you stopped the rehearsal last night."

Cliff stared at her for a long moment, his cheeks trembling with suppressed fury. Finally he yelled, "Alfred Crane!"

The small, balding man with glasses appeared from the darkness of the wings. "I'm right here, Cliff."

"Tell this girl what happens in your earth-shattering play." He raised his voice and called, "Skitch!"

The stage manager stuck her head out from behind the curtain.

"Maggie Carr will go on for Miss Can't-Make-It-to-Rehearsal-on-Time."

Maggie, who normally played the role of the housekeeper, stood up in the audience. "I'm ready, Cliff."

While the actors prepared to start the scene, Alfred Crane sat Amanda down on the couch to tell her the plot of his play. He tended to speak too quickly, which made it hard to understand him. "You know that Miss Cantwell plays Morgan Deerfield, a lady who married for money. Her stepdaughter, Eloise, played by Kitty, has returned home for her father's funeral."

"I remember," Amanda said. "I saw the dress rehearsal last night."

The shy man's eyes brightened momentarily. "Did you like it?"

"Very much so. Until the accident, that is."

"Ah, yes, the, uh . . . accident." The bright little spark disappeared from Alfred Crane's eyes. "Well." He cleared his throat awkwardly and continued. "Then you realize that everyone—Colonel Pinchmore, Morgan Deerfield, Dr. Hastings, and Mrs. Bromley, the housekeeper—they're all in on a plot to make, uh, the girl, um . . ."

"Eloise," Amanda offered.

"Yes, Eloise, thank you—to make her think she's going mad. They want to make her think she's killing everyone. Then they can have her committed, and Morgan and Dr. Hastings can live happily ever after."

"Morgan and Dr. Hastings?" Amanda repeated. The idea of Jaqueline Cantwell and Richard Tyson, the actors playing those characters, living happily ever after was very hard to believe.

"Yes, yes." The little man nodded his head quickly. "That's one of the twists. Because, of course, Morgan isn't *really* dead. Her ghost is just a device to make Eloise truly go off the deep end."

"But it doesn't work," Amanda said.

"Exactly. Eloise shoots Morgan and runs off with the doctor. So, you see, the plot twists again. We discover that the handsome doctor was *really* in on a murder plot with the stepdaughter Eloise. They needed to get rid of Jaqueline—I mean, Morgan Deerfield—to share her wealth among themselves."

Amanda nodded her head slowly, trying to follow

the complicated story. "I think I understand everything."

"Of course, it plays *much* better than I could ever tell it," the little man said apologetically. "I think. The story has one or two small glitches, but we'll work those out on the road before it goes to Broadway. All you need to do is serve the tea, and react to the second murder. Simple, really."

The day before, Amanda might have agreed with him, but as the time neared for her to actually *do* it, she was certain she wouldn't remember a thing. Especially since the director was being so mean.

"All right, Amanda," Cliff Verdery said, "take your place in the wings, stage left."

Amanda nodded and walked quickly across the stage to the other side.

"Hold it!" Cliff Verdery called out. "Where's your tea tray?"

"I don't know," Amanda answered, her patience wearing a little thin. "No one's told me where it is. And I *still* don't have a script."

"*What?* Did *everyone* check their brains at the door? Someone, *anyone*, give the girl a script!" He looked around and noticed Teddy Ballard taking his starting position by the French doors. "Teddy, you don't need yours this scene. Let her use it."

"You'd think this two-bit outfit could afford scripts," Teddy grumbled as he pulled a dog-eared script from his coat pocket and handed it to Amanda. "Use it in good health, dear, but give it back before we open this evening. I like to have it on my person at all times, in case I go up."

"Go up," Amanda repeated to herself. She assumed that meant forgetting your lines, something she knew she was certain to do. She flipped to Act Two, Scene Three, and scanned the page.

"Here is your tea, miss," she read to herself softly.

Amanda flipped a few more pages. That was all there was to her part. One line. She shut the script and moved to her place.

"Aren't you forgetting something?" the director sang out sarcastically.

"Oh, the tea tray!" Amanda spun in a circle, looking for it on the set.

"Not on the stage, dear," the director said, "*backstage,* on the prop table." As Amanda hurried off toward the wings, she heard Cliff Verdery complain to Kitty, "I thought you said she had done *lots* of plays."

"She has," Kitty said meekly. "But never in this theatre."

Cliff hung his head in his hands. "Oh, brother."

When she reached the wings, Amanda was grateful for the darkness that enveloped her. Every part of her wanted to search for the exit, but her pride was too strong. "I'll show that jerk," she whispered under her breath.

"That's the spirit," a husky voice answered beside her.

Amanda nearly jumped out of her skin. She reached out into the darkness, and her fingertips touched a face. A lock of hair brushed her hand, and a zing of electricity went through her as she realized who it was.

Mick caught her wrist with one hand and guided her to a folding table. "This is the prop table," he said. "I'll always be near it."

Amanda's eyes adjusted to the darkness, and she saw the tiny blue light bulb used to light the table. There in the center sat her tea tray.

"How did you get past the guard at the door?"

"Easy," he said, handing her the tray. "I'm the new prop assistant."

"But how did you persuade them to hire you for this?"

"Ask me no questions, and I'll tell you no lies."

"Miss Hart!"

Mick turned her toward the stage and whispered in her ear, "Knock 'em dead, kid."

Amanda strode onto the stage just as Jaqueline Cantwell appeared at the back of the auditorium. "Sorry, my darlings! Traffic was horrendous."

"Quiet in the house," Cliff Verdery shouted. "Rehearsal has already begun."

"But how can it begin without me?" Jaqueline stood in the aisle, mystified.

"Your *understudy* didn't find the traffic horrendous," Cliff replied. "She will be doing your part today."

"What?" Miss Cantwell shrieked. "That's ridiculous. We open tonight."

"You might have remembered that when you decided to arrive late."

Kitty joined Amanda on the stage. "Cliff's really telling her, isn't he?"

Amanda nodded, hoping he would have no further occasion to direct his anger at her.

"They've been like this since rehearsals began."

"Why did Jaqueline and the other producers hire him?"

"Because Cliff Verdery just happens to be the hottest director on the West Coast."

"If he's so hot, why did he take this job?"

Teddy Ballard, who had been standing behind them, entered their discussion. "Because he hasn't had a Broadway show yet, and he needs one if his career is to really take off."

Amanda shook her head. "But I don't understand why two people would work together, if they hated each other like that."

Teddy threw his head back and laughed. "My dear, if you're looking for things to make sense, you've come to the wrong place. There's no justice in the theatre, only survival of the fittest."

Richard joined their circle. "Teddy, you're lecturing again."

"*Moi?*" Teddy put one hand to his chest dramatically. "Forgive me."

"Never!" Jaqueline Cantwell's voice boomed around the theatre. "I will not watch a cheap imitation of my role. When you're prepared to hold a proper rehearsal, call for me in my dressing room."

With that, she stomped up the stairs of the stage and out through the wings, slamming every door she could get her hands on.

"Places for Scene Three," Skitch called out without skipping a beat.

"But, Cliff, darling," Teddy reasoned, "you don't really intend to rehearse without Jaqui, do you? No offense to you, Maggie, but Jaqui is the one who will be opening in the role tonight." Then he whispered loudly, "And let's face it, she needs as much rehearsal as she can get. The old girl's pretty rusty."

This solicited a thin half-smile from the director, but he wasn't to be swayed. "Let's run the apparition sequence, please."

"But that's an important scene," Teddy protested.

"Don't worry," Cliff reassured the white-haired actor. "We'll do it again with her, but I think Miss Cantwell should suffer a little first. Are you ready, Maggie?"

Maggie, who had been standing at the top of the stairs, peeked her head around the curtain. "Ready."

"Okay, let's do it." He flopped down into a front-row seat and crossed his arms.

Amanda, holding the script and tea tray, entered from stage right, set the tea tray on the table, and announced, "Here's your tea, miss."

Kitty turned and said, "Thank you, Dora." As Amanda stepped back to the sideboard, Kitty called, "It's ready, Colonel Pinchmore."

Teddy, who was positioned at the French doors, spun with a hideous expression on his face. He pretended to clutch a knife stuck in his chest. He gasped several times, and staggered about the stage. He looked so funny, Amanda wanted to laugh out loud. Then he collapsed across the couch.

At the same moment Richard Tyson, as Dr. Hastings, entered and accused Kitty of murder. She reached for the silver pistol that lay on the desk, just as Maggie appeared at the top of the stairs.

"Amanda, act scared," the director called out from the audience. "Cower in the corner, babe."

Amanda backed against the wall, doing her best terrified look. Out of the corner of her eye, she could see a dark silhouette standing in the wings. She hoped Mick wasn't laughing at her performance.

"Come down the steps, Maggie," Cliff Verdery coached, "and wave your arms in a ghostly manner."

Maggie did as she was told, intoning darkly, "Eloise, you must pay for your—*aaaiieee!*"

The dreadful howl that filled the air was real as the top step collapsed and Maggie crashed into the railing of the stairs. There was a terrible splintering sound. The banister gave way, and Maggie Carr fell to the floor with an awful thud.

CHAPTER SIX

I'll be fine," Maggie said as Mick carried her into her dressing room. "I'm just a little bruised."

Amanda brought her a glass of water and sent Pepper to find an ice pack for Maggie's rapidly swelling ankle.

"Maggie," Skitch said, coming into the dressing room, "I can dial 911, and the paramedics will be here in ten minutes."

"I don't need that," Maggie replied, smiling bravely. "Really."

Skitch shook her head. "The crew has some major explaining to do, and I mean right now!" She stepped into the hallway, and they heard her shout at the top of her lungs, "Dan Carnegie!"

Cliff Verdery stuck his head in the door. "Hey,

babe, my heart stopped cold when you went over that banister. You all right?"

"I'm fine, Cliff. If you need me to go on today, I'm sure I can do it."

The director patted her on the shoulder. "No, I want you to rest until this evening."

"But what about Jaqueline?"

"Oh, she'll do the show, I'm sure. I just wanted to make her sweat a little. Thanks, Maggie, you're a real trouper." He patted her once more and was out the door.

Maggie Carr watched him leave, and then a sob that must have been building up for a long time burst from inside her. "A real trouper," she said bitterly. "Is that all I am?"

Amanda hurriedly shut the dressing room door.

"I nearly got killed. I probably have several broken bones, and that's the thanks I get—a pat on the shoulder." Another loud sob escaped from her, and she lay her head on her hands on the dressing table. Amanda could see a huge scrape up the side of her arm where a bruise was already forming. A thin streak of blood ran down the side of her leg. "That witch! It's all her doing."

Pepper, who had arrived with the ice, asked, "Who?"

"Jaqueline Cantwell, of course. I wouldn't be surprised if she rigged that step on purpose."

"How could Jaqueline have had anything to do with it?" Pepper asked. "She was late."

"I'm sure that stair was an accident," Amanda said,

hoping her voice sounded more convincing than she felt.

"Nothing that happens with that woman is an accident. She deliberately came late today. She knew Cliff would put me in the role. She *knew* it!" Maggie pounded her fist on the table. "I could just kill her!"

Amanda knelt beside her. "Here's a couple of aspirin and a glass of water, Miss Carr."

The actress took it resignedly. Already the fire had gone out of her eyes, and her shoulders slumped miserably. "Call me Maggie—everyone else does." She leaned back into her chair and gently probed the ugly bruise with her fingers.

"Jaqui and I used to be friends. Can you believe it? We started in summer stock the same year, sharing rooms, doing a different show every week." Maggie smiled sadly. "I was the up-and-coming leading lady. Jaqui played comic maids, sidekicks, supporting roles. Then she got her hooks into George—he was already well known in the theatre—and that was it.

"She made it, and I didn't. And after twenty-five years, she still has to rub it in." Her eyes flashed suddenly. "I hate that woman!"

"I don't understand," Amanda said. "Why do you work with her?"

"Honey, you don't know much about the theatre, do you?" Maggie dabbed at her eyes with a tissue. "An actor is out of work ninety percent of the time. You can't afford to turn down a job."

A light tap sounded on the door and she said, "Come in."

Richard Tyson leaned around the doorsill and grinned. "I'm glad you're okay, Maggie."

"Thanks, Richard."

"It's just too bad Miss Can't-Act-Well wasn't on those stairs. I'd have loved to see her fall flat on her face."

Maggie chuckled, then winced and felt her ribs. Richard's expression changed. "Don't you think you should see a doctor?"

Maggie shook her head violently.

"Well, keep your chin up, kid."

As Richard was leaving, Teddy stuck his head in the door. "Maggie, dear heart, there are much easier ways to get applause. Next time, call for your stunt double." He looked over both shoulders, then reached into his leather bag and pulled out a small silver flask. "Here, take a sip of this. It will make your pain much more tolerable."

"Which pain?" she asked, unscrewing the top. "Physical, or mental?"

"Both."

Amanda realized that whatever was in the flask was probably responsible for the constant rosiness of Teddy's cheeks. Maggie took a swig from the silver flask, then handed it back to the older actor.

"We must all be on our guard," Teddy warned. "This show is cursed."

"*Cursed?*" Alfred Crane, the playwright, peered out from behind him. "Oh, Teddy, please don't say that." He took off his glasses and nervously polished them on his shirt. "All of this is very bad publicity for the play."

"Bad?" Teddy raised one white, fluffy eyebrow. "Quite the contrary, old sport, it's the *best* thing that could happen. This play is in the headlines every day. People are dying to see what ghoulish thing's going to happen next."

Alfred shook his head. "I don't like that. It could backfire and close the show."

"Don't worry, Alfred."

"I *have* to worry. Ten years ago George Cantwell died on opening night, and my play has never been done since."

"Yes, Jaqueline made sure of that."

"What?" Alfred Crane's eyes were two big saucers. "I didn't know that."

"Oh, dear, I thought everyone knew. Especially you, the playwright, of all people."

Amanda couldn't keep from asking, "How could she keep his play from being done?"

"Alfred sold her the rights to it," Teddy replied.

The playwright shook his head in disbelief. "But she told me no one in the business would touch the play because a curse had been put on it."

Teddy took a sip from his flask. "Yes, and the curse was named Jaqueline Cantwell. She was determined that no theatre would do *Murder at Midnight* until she was out of mourning." He grimaced and added, "Who would've thought she'd mourn old Georgie for ten years?"

"Oh, this is terrible!" The playwright slumped in

the chair next to Maggie. "All this time I thought she was my friend. I've spent ten years of my life waiting, waiting for this play to be produced."

"I'm sure she thought she was doing you a big favor, saving it for her comeback," Teddy said. "It's just like Jaqui to think that."

"I feel absolutely awful. I've never felt so bad in my life." Alfred took the bottle of aspirin that was sitting on the table and popped three of them in his mouth.

"Don't feel too bad, Alfred, at least *Murder*'s being done." Maggie patted him on the back. "You've finally gotten your break."

Amanda could tell by the way she said it that Maggie felt her big break had come and gone long ago. There was more bruised about Maggie Carr than her knees and elbows.

Mick appeared at the door. He motioned for Amanda and Pepper to follow him. They left Maggie, Alfred, and Teddy to console each other and followed him up into the backstage area.

"Mick, where are we going?" Amanda asked.

He put one finger to his lips and mimed that the walls had ears. Then he climbed the circular staircase to the floor above the stage. A red door marked "Prop Room" stood slightly ajar. They followed him through the door into an incredible world of make-believe.

The room was packed from floor to ceiling with chairs, tables, and couches of all different styles. One wall was lined with Roman shields, stage swords, and daggers. A *papier-mâché* rhinoceros head hung on another wall next to a trick bicycle built for three. One whole shelf was filled with teapots, with matching cups and saucers. Amanda and Pepper wanted to stop and explore, but Mick shook his head. He led them over to a heavy metal door marked "Exit."

Mick gave the door a shove, and brilliant daylight streamed into the room. He stepped out into the afternoon air, and Pepper and Amanda joined him, leaving the door behind them slightly open.

"Now we can talk," Mick said. They were standing on a rusted fire escape two stories above the stage door. The only thing facing them was the redbrick exterior of the building across the alley.

Pepper peered over the railing of the rickety metal staircase and announced, "I demand a safety net."

Mick chuckled. "It seems wobbly, but don't worry—it's safe."

"Famous last words," Pepper retorted. "I'm not trusting anything connected to this building."

"That's smart," Mick said, "but I wouldn't blame it on the theatre. Someone is behind all this."

"What did you find out?" Amanda asked, inching closer to the door. She wanted to be able to hop inside if anything gave way.

"First of all, that accident on the stairs was no accident. The nails had been removed from the step, and someone sawed halfway through the railing."

"Just enough to make it look safe but give way at the slightest pressure," Amanda concluded.

"Right."

"Are they planning to tell the cast?" Amanda asked.

Mick shook his head. "Skitch said if we tell the cast,

then we have to tell the police. If we tell the police, then *Murder at Midnight* is dead in the water."

"But what about everyone's safety?"

"That doesn't seem to worry her, or anyone else. All they care about is getting the show through opening tonight." Mick ran his hand through his hair. "So I've come to a decision."

"What's that, Mick?" Amanda looked into his intense blue eyes.

"You're quitting this play."

"What?" Amanda stepped backward and nearly fell over the side of the fire escape.

"Careful!" Mick reached out to steady her.

Amanda gripped the railing. "Are you serious?"

"Of course I'm serious," Mick replied. "People are getting hurt around here."

Amanda sputtered, "But what gives you the right to make my decisions for me?"

"I have every right."

"Since when?"

"Since I signed on to look after you." Mick folded his arms across his chest. "Well, I'm looking, and from this angle, things look lousy."

"Well, from *this* angle, things look just fine," Amanda said, folding her own arms and glaring back at him.

"Doesn't anybody care what my angle looks like?" Pepper asked.

"No!" Amanda and Mick shouted at her.

"Hey, chill out, guys." Pepper backed up against the fire escape door. "I think we're all a little rattled by these accidents. Maybe we should reexamine the situation."

"That's what I'm trying to tell Miss Hart here, but she doesn't seem to want to listen to common sense."

"I'm listening," Amanda retorted. "But who's making sense? You walk in here and start ordering me around."

"Look, Amanda, I don't know what's going on here, but it's not good." Mick sat on the railing, balancing above the grate. "I just don't want to see you get hurt."

Amanda took a deep breath and tried to calm her nerves. "I'm sorry, but I can't quit. The play opens tonight. Not only is Kitty counting on me, but so are a lot of other people."

Pepper crossed her arms and stared at her suspiciously. "Are you sure you haven't been bitten by the I-wanta-be-a-star bug?"

"Positive," Amanda said. "Besides, I signed a contract and I'm stuck."

"Mandy, there's a maniac loose," Mick said. "And we've got to stop him."

"I think we should stick together," Pepper said. "This whole theatre is an accident waiting to happen. Everywhere you turn around there's an electric cable lying loose, or a heavy wall barely attached to a support."

Mick hopped off the top railing, and the fire escape bounced wildly. Pepper clutched at Amanda, who threw her arms around Mick.

"If this is what you mean by sticking together," Mick said, chuckling, "I like it."

Then the bolt holding one side of the fire escape to the brick wall broke with a loud snap, and the entire landing swung about a foot away from the wall. They looked at each other, eyes wide with fear.

"Oh, no!" Pepper moaned in fear. "It's going to break away."

Suddenly voices sounded on the other side of the door. Mick put one arm around Amanda and whispered, "Don't move!"

CHAPTER SEVEN

Amanda held her breath and listened. Her head rested against Mick's chest, and she could feel the pounding of his heart. She was certain hers was going twice as fast. His flannel shirt felt soft against her cheek, and he smelled good, like fresh, clean soap.

"This curse business has gone too far," a voice said angrily on the other side of the door. "Every time the tiniest thing goes wrong at this theatre, it hits the front page of the *Chronicle*."

Through the crack in the door, Amanda could see Cliff Verdery waving a newspaper. "I just got a call from Fred Shaefer at the city desk. He already knows about the stairs collapsing! How is this happening?"

Skitch stepped into Amanda's line of vision. "The

day after the first accident Miss Cantwell ordered me to call the publicity department the minute anything unusual happened."

"I'll just bet she did." Cliff slammed the newspaper on the table. "Miss Cantwell has gotten more coverage in the last two weeks than she's had in the last ten years."

"I'm sorry, Cliff," Skitch said, "but she is one of the producers of this play. I have to do what she says."

"Including rigging those stairs?" Cliff asked quietly.

Skitch took a step backward. "What do you mean?"

"It seems a little strange to me that the stairs collapse, Jaqueline's understudy takes the fall, and *she* gets all of the publicity."

"Hey, hold it," Skitch said angrily. "I had nothing to do with that accident. And why would you think Jaqueline rigged that step?"

"To get her name in the paper." Cliff threw up his hands. "The woman is desperate. She needs all the public sympathy she can get. If this play isn't a hit, her career is finished. She knows it, and I know it. That's why she hates me."

Skitch paced in a circle, shaking her head. "Are you saying she had something to do with all of the accidents?"

Cliff nodded his head. "I'd bet anything that she did."

Skitch put her hands on her hips and faced Cliff. "Then what are you going to do?"

"Do? I'd like to kill the woman!" He slammed his fist against one of the stacks of chairs in the room.

They hit the floor with a crash. "Nobody, I mean, *nobody* tampers with one of my shows and lives to tell about it."

"Should we cancel the show?"

The director ran his fingers through his hair and took a long, deep breath. "No, I've worked too hard to get this break to have Jaqueline Cantwell mess it up. We'll finish rehearsal this afternoon as planned. And we'll open this show tonight, come hell or high water."

"What if she pulls something else?" Skitch asked.

"I don't think she will," Cliff replied. "Jaqueline wanted publicity for the opening, and she got it. But just to be on the safe side, keep a close eye on things this evening."

Skitch nodded.

"Now call the cast and crew onstage. We've got a lot of work to do."

They left the prop room, and there was a deadly stillness. No one on the fire escape moved.

"Jaqueline Cantwell," Amanda breathed softly. "That's amazing."

Mick nodded. "It fits. All of it."

"Wow," Pepper said. "It's weird to think she'd screw up her show just to make the headlines."

"Do you think Cliff is right," Amanda asked, "that she won't try anything else?"

"It's a good bet." Mick held Amanda at arm's length and looked into her eyes. "Just the same, stay away from her. Don't talk to her, don't sit by her, don't let her know you exist."

Pepper tapped her on the shoulder and said, "Ditto."

"And after the opening, I'll tell Kitty," Amanda said. "She'll have to decide for herself whether she wants to stay on."

"What about you?" Mick asked.

Amanda grinned. "My theatrical career will be one of the shortest in history. Here tonight, gone tomorrow."

Mick smiled with obvious relief and gently squeezed her shoulder. Amanda felt a warm glow spread across her body.

"All this togetherness is very cute," Pepper interjected, "but do either of you have any idea of how we're going to get off this fire escape in one piece?"

Mick nodded. "Very carefully."

As if to punctuate her point, the metal structure shifted with a groan, and Amanda and Pepper both flung themselves against Mick once again.

"Go easy, ladies," he said softly. "And we'll be just fine."

He reached around behind them with one hand and gently opened the door into the prop room. The metal door clanged against the inner wall, and the fire escape tilted precariously. Pepper grabbed Amanda's hand, and they stepped through the door at the same time. Mick was right behind them.

"Okay, I admit it," Pepper moaned. "That was *really* scary."

"I better put a No Exit sign there," Mick said. "So no one gets hurt."

Pepper suddenly gasped. "You don't think Jaqueline Cantwell had anything to do with that fire escape, do you?"

"No." Mick laughed. "She may be devious, but she couldn't rig this entire theatre. It'd be impossible."

Amanda wanted to laugh with him, but she couldn't. "I hope you're right."

Suddenly the loudspeaker backstage crackled and Skitch's voice could be heard saying, "Amanda Hart. Onstage, please."

"Omigosh! I'm late for rehearsal." Amanda jumped and ran out of the prop room and down the circular staircase as fast as she could.

"Where've you been?" Cliff Verdery barked as she rushed onto the set from the wings. Amanda opened her mouth to reply but he cut her off. "Never mind. Get in place for the apparition."

"Hold it, folks!" Dan Carnegie called from offstage. "I'm having some problems with the fog machine."

"So what else is new?" Richard Tyson sighed. "This whole theatre is falling apart."

"I'll try to fix it as soon as I can."

Cliff Verdery threw up his hands. "Is anyone aware that we open in less than five hours?"

Jaqueline Cantwell lit a cigarette and exhaled. "We're aware. I don't think the crew is."

Cliff pointedly ignored her remark and shouted into the wings, "Dan, do you have any idea how long this will take?"

"Nope, sorry."

"Well." Cliff took a couple of deep breaths. "Let's practice the apparition scene anyway—*sans* fog. Jaqueline, take your place at the top of the stairs."

Jaqueline Cantwell didn't move. She just stood center stage, smoking her cigarette.

"Miss Cantwell," Skitch called. "The director would like to rehearse the apparition scene."

"I heard him, dear. I'm not deaf." Jaqueline turned to face the director. "Look, Cliff, I'm not using those stairs until I'm certain they're safe."

Cliff Verdery spun around so quickly that for a moment Amanda was sure he was going to attack her. Then he pressed his palms over his eyes for what seemed an endless amount of time. Finally he looked up at her and said in a voice that was deathly calm, "You and I both know they're just fine, don't we?"

"And what's that supposed to mean?"

"It means that *you* have nothing to worry about," he replied. "It's the *rest* of the cast who have to worry."

She stopped in midpuff, then briskly stubbed out her cigarette. "If you're accusing me of something, Verdery, I think you had better come right out with it. Quit pussyfooting around."

"All right." The director marched over to the table and, grabbing the copy of the newspaper he'd shown to Skitch, waved it under her nose. "I'm saying you caused all of these so-called accidents, just to generate some publicity to feed your pathetic ego." There was a startled gasp from the rest of the company.

"How *dare* you!" The actress drew herself up to her

full height and thundered, "Are you forgetting *who* drank that contaminated cup of tea, *who* was meant to turn on that lamp, *who* was supposed to fall down those stairs? Me!"

"Oh, yes, you're awfully clever. The bleach in that tea was such a minute quantity, it didn't hurt you a bit. And remember, Miss Cantwell, you're the one who told Sally Quince to turn on the lamp at that moment. And you knew I would make Maggie rehearse in your place, because I warned you weeks ago that I'd put your understudy on if you were ever late again."

"That's a perfectly dreadful thing for you to say. It's even worse that you could think it." Jaqueline stood up and faced the cast. "I would never hurt anyone in this show." Her voice shook with emotion. "You are my comrades. We depend on each other. Oh, we may have our disagreements, but at heart we all love each other."

"Save it for the ticket holders, Jaqui," Cliff Verdery muttered. "It won't wash with this group."

Behind Jaqueline's back, Richard Tyson rolled his eyes at Kitty Butterfield, who giggled nervously. Jaqueline turned so hard at the sound she nearly fell over.

"How dare you laugh at me, you little amateur!" Her lips curled up into a sneer.

All the color drained from Kitty's face. "But I wasn't laughing at you—"

Jaqueline cut her off. "You're not an actress, you're nothing but a model!"

Kitty looked like she'd been hit in the face, and Amanda's heart went out to her.

"Stop staring at me," Jaqueline snapped. "Either speak up or go back to your corner, where you belong."

Kitty's chin quivered, and she cried out, "You're just awful! I wish you were dead!"

Tears sprang to her eyes, and she ran from the stage.

"Satisfied?" Cliff said, pointing in Kitty's direction. "Is this the way you treat your 'comrades'? With insults? You've picked away at her relentlessly, from the beginning. You won't be content until you've humiliated or destroyed everyone in the cast. Well, I for one have *had* it with you."

"Now, Cliff, my boy, aren't we being a trifle harsh?" Teddy spoke up. "I mean, the girl did laugh at Jaqueline."

"Thank you, Teddy. It's reassuring to know I have *some* friends, but I can handle this situation myself." Jaqueline shouted at Skitch, "Get the other producers on the phone!" She marched over to her purse and lit another cigarette. "I should have done this a long time ago."

"What are you up to now?" Cliff demanded.

She blew the smoke out her nose and smiled. "I'm about to have you fired."

"You can't fire me," he shouted, "because I quit. Get *that* in the newspapers!"

He threw the newspaper at her feet, then marched up the center aisle, with Skitch running after him.

"Good riddance to bad rubbish," Jaqueline shouted. "And if you ever step foot in this theatre again, Verdery, I'll have you arrested!"

Alfred Crane, who had been quiet throughout the argument, hissed at Jaqueline, "You'll regret this!" Then he scurried up the aisle after Skitch and the director.

No one said a word for a moment. Finally, Jaqueline Cantwell murmured, "Oh, well. I suppose we're all under a lot of stress." She put one hand to her forehead. "I have a splitting headache. If anyone wants me, I'll be in my dressing room." She left the stage without a backward glance.

"My, my, my," Teddy said, clapping his hands. "Looks like we're on our own tonight, my darlings."

"If I didn't have film directors flying in from L.A.," Richard Tyson said, "I'd go to the union about these accidents. As it is, well . . . I'm keeping on my guard. I suggest all of you do the same."

Maggie nodded. "I intend to stay in my dressing room whenever I'm not onstage."

The lobby doors flipped open, and Skitch stood framed against the light from outside. "As you can see, this rehearsal is over. We do have an opening tonight, so I expect to see you all back here at seven-thirty for an eight o'clock 'Go.' By then, I hope, this whole mess will be straightened out."

The strain was starting to show in Skitch's voice, but Amanda admired the way the stage manager was handling the crisis. She seemed to be the only one in the whole organization capable of self-control.

Jonathan and Maggie nodded and left the stage. Teddy turned to follow when he noticed Amanda standing motionless by the sideboard. He paused by the curtain and said, "Don't worry, love, it will all work out just fine."

"Don't worry?" Amanda shook her head in amazement. "Horrible accidents are happening to everyone, Jaqueline Cantwell has destroyed whatever confidence Kitty had left, the director has quit, and I've only practiced my part once. Don't worry?"

At that moment, Dan Carnegie stepped onto the stage with a wrench in his hand. "I fixed the fog machine. The darn thing was missing a washer. We can go on with the rehearsal."

Teddy leaned over to Amanda and whispered, "And that, my dear, is what's known in the theatre as bad timing."

CHAPTER EIGHT

A manda stared at her reflection in the mirror on her bedroom door. In less than two hours she would make her theatrical debut—and she was not ready. Amanda cleared her throat and spoke her line from the play.

"Here is your *tea*, miss."

She frowned and tried again.

"Here is *your* tea, miss."

Amanda shook her head. "That's awful." She plastered a huge smile on her face. "*Here* is your tea, miss."

Applause sounded from behind her, and she turned to see her cousin, Josh, smirking at her from the doorway to her bedroom. "Have you tried 'Here is your tea, *miss*?'"

Amanda raised a threatening fist at her fourteen-year-old cousin. "Don't laugh, Josh! I have to get up in front of two thousand people tonight and talk. I'd like to see you try it."

Josh blushed, turning his freckles and the tips of his ears a bright pink. "I'm sorry, Mandy. You just looked so funny standing in front of the mirror, saying that one line over and over."

Amanda sighed. "I don't feel very funny. I feel terrified."

"I know a way to calm you down," he said. "But you have to do as I say."

"What?" Amanda asked impatiently. "I have to leave for the theatre any minute."

"Face the mirror."

Amanda turned to look at her reflection. A girl dressed in black-and-gray-striped silk pants, a starched white shirt, and black velvet bolero jacket stared back at her. She adjusted the black bow tie and took a deep breath to quiet her nerves.

"Okay," Amanda declared. "I'm facing the mirror."

"Now repeat after me." Josh stepped behind her and watched her intently in the mirror. "Madame, your limousine is here."

Amanda rolled her eyes impatiently. "Madame, your limo—" She stopped midsentence and turned to look at Josh. "Are you serious?"

He pointed to the window. "Would I lie?"

Amanda rushed to the window.

Sitting in front of her house was a gleaming black limousine. The driver leaned against the open front door. He was a muscular, dark-haired guy with a heavily pockmarked face, one that would scare anyone if they ran into him in a dark alley.

Amanda threw open the window. "Gabe!" she shouted. "What are you doing here?"

Gabriel Sanchez was Mick's best friend and a partner in his messenger service. He looked tough as nails but was a teddy bear at heart. When Gabe spotted Amanda, his face creased into a big, friendly smile.

"Say, hey!" Gabe gestured to the sleek limousine. "Need a ride?"

"I'll be right there!" Amanda raced to her dresser and squirted a dash of perfume behind each ear. Then for luck, she slipped on a tiny pearl ring that her parents had given her when she turned sixteen. She paused just long enough to kiss her cousin on the cheek, then ran down the stairs and out the front door.

"Break a leg!" Josh shouted from the upstairs window.

"Thanks!" Amanda called back. Then she remembered all the accidents that had happened, and added, "I think."

"*Hola, guapa!*" Gabe said, opening the back door of the limousine.

Amanda hugged him warmly. "Gabe, it's sure good to see you!"

"Likewise," he replied with a grin.

"Where's Mick?" Amanda asked, looking around. A hand reached out from the backseat and pulled her by the arm into the black leather interior. Gabe bent down and asked, "That answer your question?"

He shut the door and hopped into the driver's seat. Mick, who was dressed in a silver-gray striped suit with black shirt and skinny tie, said, "I figured, for your opening, you should go in style."

"But how did you get the limo?"

"Gabe does chauffeuring on the side and got hired as Richard Tyson's driver. He'll drop us off and then go get Tyson."

Gabe slid open the glass divider and asked, "All set?"

Mick nodded. "Let it happen, Captain."

The limousine pulled away from the curb, and Amanda leaned back in the plush seat. This was certainly going to be a night to remember.

"I wanted to spend a little time with you alone," Mick said in his husky voice. Amanda's heart raced suddenly, until he added, "To talk about Jaqueline Cantwell, and tonight."

By the even tone of his voice she could tell Mick was all business, and she forced herself to be that way, too. "Okay," she said. "Have you learned anything new?"

Mick held up the evening edition of the newspaper. He flipped to the entertainment section. The advertisement for the opening night of *Murder at Midnight* was overshadowed by the headline "Director Fired from Cursed Play—Actress Vows to Go On."

Amanda whistled softly. "Wow. That was fast."

Mick nodded. "Too fast. I think that headline was phoned in before the firing ever happened."

"You mean Jaqueline Cantwell planned to fire Cliff from the start?"

"Dan Carnegie said those two have never gotten along. He also told me that Miss Cantwell had a reputation for firing directors. It was almost expected."

"Like a theatre tradition?" Amanda sat forward in the seat. That explained why Teddy and the others in the cast hadn't been very concerned about Cliff Verdery's dismissal.

"Yeah, ol' Cliff was given a real sucker punch." Mick tucked the newspaper in a pocket on the door. "She set him up, and down he went."

"I'm glad I'm only in this for tonight," Amanda said with relief. "I don't think I could take the craziness. It would have to rub off on you."

Before she knew it, Gabe had parked the limousine in front of the Gateway Theatre and was holding the door open. A few audience members had already arrived, and Amanda could tell by their excited murmurs that they were wondering just which stars she and Mick were. Mick was obviously loving it. He looped his arm through hers, waved at the crowd, and ushered her through the stage door.

Inside the theatre a sense of nervous anticipation seemed to have infected everyone. Even the guard at the door was in uniform, and for once his feet weren't resting on the top of his desk. The crew completed their preshow checks backstage, speaking in hushed tones. The huge velvet curtain was stretched across the front of the stage. Amanda looked at it and shivered. The next time she stood on the set, two thousand faces would be watching her every move.

Mick escorted her to the stairs and said, "After you get dressed, join me at the prop table. I'll have a chair ready for you."

Amanda nodded without really hearing him. She could feel her body going numb with fear again. As she passed through the green room, she was shocked to find the room full of people already in costume. Then she realized that these were the party guests who appeared at the top of the first act. They hadn't been at the rehearsal that afternoon.

Alfred Crane was slumped on the couch, muttering to himself over and over again, "How could she do this to me?"

"Mr. Crane?" Amanda kneeled beside him. "Are you all right?"

He raised his balding head and peered at her with bloodshot eyes. "Of course I'm all right. It's my play that's in trouble. Something awful's going to happen."

Amanda could tell he had been drinking. "What will happen to your play?" she asked gently.

"The same thing that happened ten years ago," he moaned. "She'll keep it from being produced. And I'll remain a nonentity." Hatred lit up his eyes as he pointed toward Jaqueline Cantwell's dressing room. "I thought she was my friend."

"Now, Alfred, is that any way to talk?" Teddy Ballard eased himself into one of the tattered armchairs.

"Amanda will think we theatre people are callous beasts."

"Aren't we?" Alfred focused one bloodshot eye on Teddy. "No loyalty, no decency, no nothing. Always looking out for Number One. Your best friend is whoever can get you the next job."

"But that's what makes life interesting," Teddy joked. "The intrigues, the petty manipulations—"

"Tell the truth," Alfred interrupted. "Wouldn't you rather be playing Richard Tyson's role?"

For a moment Teddy looked away uncomfortably. Then he smiled. "Well, of course."

"Didn't you think Jaqui should have given it to you?" Alfred persisted. "After all you've been to her, she owes it to you."

Amanda's eyes widened.

Teddy smiled at her reaction. "Yes, dear, we all go way back. Alfred, Jaqui, and I tried to open this show ten years ago, but George's accident prevented us." He patted Alfred Crane on the knee confidently. "But not this time. The show *will* go on, and it will be a triumph."

"I wish I could be as certain as you," Alfred replied, slurring his words together. "It . . . it just doesn't feel right."

Teddy stood up. "I think it's you who doesn't feel right." He grabbed Alfred by the elbow and pulled the little man to his feet. "Come on, we'll splash some water on your face and you'll feel much better."

Alfred nodded. Teddy whispered to Amanda over the playwright's shoulder, "Poor Alfred never could hold his liquor. He was just like this on opening night ten years ago."

"Fifteen minutes to places," Skitch's voice boomed over the monitor. "Please check your props, everyone."

Kitty stepped out of her dressing room and shrieked, "Dresser!"

Pepper stuck her head out of the costume shop. She was wearing the same uniform as the other wardrobe people, a blue smock with safety pins fastened to the shoulder.

"Amanda," she hissed. "Can you help her? I'm trying to sew a button back on this silly costume. I can't even get the needle threaded!"

Amanda nodded and rushed over to Kitty's dressing room. The young actress was hurriedly trying to apply nail polish. "It's about time," she snapped. "How long do I—oh, Amanda! I thought you were someone else."

Amanda was stunned by Kitty's behavior. "Is that the way you talk to Pepper?"

Kitty put the brush back in the bottle of nail polish and sighed. "I'm sorry. Of course not. It's just that tonight I can't seem to do anything right."

"Well, what did you want?"

"The back of my hair is messed up and my nails are all wet. Would you fix it for me?"

Amanda picked up the brush and ran it carefully through her friend's hair. "Feeling a little nervous?"

Kitty bobbed her head up and down. "Nervous isn't

the word for it. Teddy told me that Mel Bloom from Triple Star is out there."

"Is that important?"

Kitty looked at Amanda like she was out of her mind. "Triple Star is only *the* biggest casting agency in Hollywood." She held out her hand. "Look at that. My hand shakes when I just mention the name."

Somehow, seeing her friend so upset calmed Amanda. She was glad she had so little to do in the play.

"Five minutes," Skitch announced over the speaker.

"Five?" Kitty leaped up and grabbed the brush from Amanda. "I have to be alone now."

Amanda barely made it out of the dressing room before the door was shut in her face. She stared at the closed door in dismay. Kitty hardly seemed like the same person anymore. At Sutter, she had been a fun-loving senior, unpretentious and friendly. Now she was behaving like a temperamental starlet. Amanda shrugged her shoulders. "I hope it's just nerves," she mumbled to herself.

She checked her watch. Her entrance wasn't until the second act, which gave her lots of time to get dressed. Amanda decided to take Mick's suggestion and get ready early. That way she could watch all of the action from backstage.

Amanda slipped into her dressing room and was startled to find several bouquets of flowers lying on her makeup table. There was a Boston fern from Miss Wilson on behalf of the academy. Nearby lay a bouquet of roses from her aunt and uncle and Josh. A dazzling arrangement of irises lay beside her hand mirror. She picked them up and read the card inside.

"Knock 'em dead, kid! —M. S." Amanda smiled as a warm flush reddened her face. "Mick," she whispered softly. She put the flowers into a glass of water and hurried to get ready.

It didn't take Amanda long. She pulled her hair into a French twist on her head, then pinned the white lace cap to her hair. She slipped easily into the maid's costume, which now fit her like a glove. The black silk stockings underneath the short skirt made her smile. They *did* make her legs look nice. Of course, the high heels helped. She had already applied her makeup at home. She was checking her hair for the fifth time when the loudspeaker crackled again.

"Places, everybody," Skitch said. "Places for the top of the show." There was slight pause and the stage manager added, "Let's make it a good one."

Amanda felt her pulse quicken at the announcement. She raced down the tunnel and reached the stage just as the lights were dimming. They went completely to black and the swoosh of the rising curtain was the only sound she heard. But Amanda wasn't really paying attention. She was trying to decipher the last image she had seen as the lights went out.

A man, dressed in black, had passed under the exit sign, and his sun-bleached hair caught the light. His profile was familiar, but she instinctively knew he was out of place.

"Cliff Verdery!" she gasped. The director who had been fired and told never to step foot in that theatre again!

CHAPTER NINE

There was a sudden rustle of movement in the dark beside her, and Amanda almost leaped out of her skin.

A husky voice chuckled. "A little jumpy tonight?"

"Mick!" Amanda whispered as her eyes adjusted to the dim light backstage. "A little."

Then Amanda remembered the bouquet of flowers Mick had sent her. "Thanks," she murmured shyly.

Mick raised an eyebrow. "What for?"

"The irises. They're my favorite flower."

A pleased smile lit up his face. "Somehow, they just seemed right, y'know?" As they looked into each other's eyes, the tension and excitement of the theatre seemed far away. It was just the two of them, standing together in the half-light.

Mick cleared his throat abruptly. "I'm glad you liked them."

She started to tell him about Cliff Verdery when the lights flared up on the stage. The audience burst into applause as the rich interior of Farley Manor was revealed. Richard Tyson stood in front of the massive fireplace with his back to the audience.

"How did he get out there so fast?" Amanda whispered. "It was pitch black."

"Glow tape." Mick held up a roll of tape that gave off a lime-green glimmer in the darkness. "I put it there myself."

"Where?" From where Amanda was standing she couldn't see any bright green glow on the stage.

"They're little tiny squares, stapled to the back of the table and couch. In the darkness, it looks like a runway. But only the actors can see it."

"How do you know so much about the theatre?" Amanda asked, realizing once again that she really knew very little about Mick.

"I've got relatives in the stagehands' union. They taught me the ropes."

There was a round of applause as Richard Tyson turned to face the audience and they recognized the former television star. He dipped his head slightly and smiled.

Just then Jaqueline Cantwell swept onto the stage through the double doors and the audience greeted her with an even louder ovation. The smile froze on Richard Tyson's face as he watched Jaqueline turn and graciously bow her head. As she turned back to

Richard to continue the play, the actress shot him a look that seemed to say, "So there!"

Off to the left of the prop table, Amanda spotted Kitty preparing for her entrance. She paced in a little circle by the French doors, humming under her breath and shaking her hands to release the tension. She seemed oblivious to the dialogue onstage. Suddenly she stopped, put a radiant smile on her face, and threw open the French doors.

"Doctor," she sang out, "I've just had the most wonderful walk in the garden!"

It was an amazing transformation. The nervous teenager backstage was now a confident young woman striding purposefully into the light of the stage. It was almost as if Kitty had stepped out of her own skin and completely into the character of Eloise. The thought that a person could be so different at the drop of a hat was a little disturbing to Amanda. How would you know if someone was being *real* or just playing another character?

Off to the right of the prop table, Amanda heard Skitch talking softly into a headset. She was perched on a high stool behind a podium that held the prompt book. "Ready on seven. And . . . go. Stand by for eight and nine."

The numbers were confusing, but each time Skitch said "Go," the lights on the stage would change, or a sound cue, like a doorbell or the radio, would be heard.

Maggie Carr, in her costume as Mrs. Bromley, the housekeeper, appeared at the prop table, and Mick handed her the feather duster. "How're you feeling?" he whispered.

"Bruised, but okay," she replied with a grimace. "I'd feel much better if I could ram this down Jaqueline's throat."

"That's more like it, Maggie," Teddy said as he joined them. He was resplendent in his colonel's uniform, with gold braid dangling from his epaulets. "Let the old bag have it."

"I thought you two were friends," Amanda said.

"We are," Teddy replied, "but that doesn't mean I like her."

Maggie chuckled, and Teddy nudged her casually with his elbow. "Announce me, dear," he said. "We're on."

The actress's eyes grew huge, and she scurried through the French doors onto the stage. "Madame," they heard her say, "Colonel Pinchmore is here to see you."

"Show him in." Jaqueline's voice reverberated back.

Teddy turned to Amanda and said, "The secret to a good entrance is to delay just long enough for the audience to focus solidly on the door." After a second he grinned. "That's long enough." With that, Teddy strolled through the French doors onto the stage.

Amanda shook her head. "He's amazing!"

Richard exited moments after Teddy's entrance. He walked calmly into the wings and held out his arms. Two ladies from wardrobe appeared, along with Pepper. They slipped off his coat and unbuttoned his shirt. While they worked, Richard whispered to

Skitch, "Look, I need more light on the couch. It's supposed to be a sunny afternoon. It feels like the middle of the night."

Skitch nodded as she spoke into her headset, "Stand by on twenty-seven."

Richard stepped into a pair of slippers that Pepper placed beside him and hissed, "And the radio cue was all wrong. The music came on before I even touched the dial."

Pepper handed Richard a comb, which he ran through his hair.

"Twenty-seven, go," Skitch said. At the same moment the phone onstage rang.

Richard tossed Pepper the comb as he shouted toward the stage, "I'll get it. I'm expecting a call from London." He stepped back into the light and picked up the receiver. The phone continued ringing. He shot a withering look into the wings and then said, "Farley Manor."

"I told him two rings," Skitch whispered to no one in particular. "But he insists on grabbing the phone on one." She sighed, then ordered over the headset, "Change the cue. He'll probably wait for two tomorrow night. Oh, well."

Pepper joined Amanda by the prop table. "Wow, that quick change was scary. My hands were shaking the whole time."

"You did great, Pepper," Amanda said, patting her on the arm. "But he could have done some of that himself, couldn't he?"

Pepper shook her head. "It goes much faster if he

just stands there. At least, that's what they tell me. It took only fifteen seconds, you know."

"Boy, this is enough material for a couple of articles in the *Spectator*," Amanda said.

"I've made an important discovery about myself," Pepper declared. "And I think it will make a good article."

"What?" Amanda giggled. "Have you been bitten by the theatre bug?"

"No way!" Pepper pushed her glasses up on her nose with a grimace. "I have discovered that I can't sew, I'm lousy with hair, I don't like hanging up clothes for other people, and I *hate* being ordered around. In short, I am about the worst person they could find for this job."

"Don't sweat it, Pep," Mick said with a grin. "After tonight, it'll all be just a bad dream."

"What happens after tonight?" Pepper asked.

"The show will play without a hitch," Amanda said. "With any luck, it will be a huge success. And we'll go back to being regular students at Sutter."

"And I'll go back to Fleet Street," Mick added.

"So you're just going to let Jaqueline Cantwell get away with all of those accidents she staged?" Pepper asked.

"Remember," Amanda reminded her friend, "we don't have a shred of proof linking Jaqueline to any of them."

"She needed an audience," Mick said. "And she got one. I just heard this turkey is sold out for the next three weeks."

"I'll still keep my distance from her, thank you very much," Pepper sniffed.

"But, Pepper, you're completely armed," Amanda teased. "Scissors, safety pins—she won't come near you."

Pepper checked her list in her pocket. "Oops, I'd better run. I have to help Kitty into her evening gown and then get ready for the *really* quick change during the second act."

The first act curtain came down to enthusiastic applause. As the actors filed by the prop table on their way back to their dressing rooms, they patted each other happily on the shoulder, murmuring how well things were going. Now they were relaxed and jovial.

But not Amanda. When Skitch called places for the beginning of Act Two, Amanda felt the cold grip of fear seize her entire body. The auditorium grew dark, the lights onstage brightened, and the second act began. There was no ignoring it now. In only a matter of minutes she would have to step onto that stage and, somehow, survive.

"Make way!" The wardrobe ladies appeared at the side of the stage, gesturing for her to move. They were carrying Jaqueline's white dress, a white latex mask, and a gold-and-white shield that fit over the front of the dress.

"Amanda!" Skitch whispered. "Stand by for your entrance."

"Mick!" Amanda hissed in a panic. "Something's happening to me. I'm a mass of jelly!"

"Stage fright," he said with a grin. "Don't worry. It

happens to everyone—even people who have been
doing it for years."

"I . . . I don't think I can hold the tea tray."

"Sure you can." Mick lifted the platter and handed
it to her. Amanda's hands were shaking so badly that
the cups clattered against the saucers, and the silver
service rattled loudly against the tray.

"Oh, no!" Amanda set it down roughly on the prop
table. "This is too humiliating! I can't walk across the
stage sounding like that."

"Believe me, no one will hear you."

"Are you kidding?" Amanda exclaimed.

"Sssh!" Skitch hushed from behind the console.
Amanda whispered hoarsely, "Are you kidding? Look
at this." She picked up the tray again, and it rattled
even louder. "Isn't there anything we can do to stop
that?"

Mick examined the tray closely. "I've got an idea.
In the meantime, take a few deep breaths."

"What are you going to do?"

"Trust me." Mick grinned confidently. "Does anyone have to use this stuff again?"

Amanda shook her head. "I just walk out there, set
the tray on the table, and say my line—" Amanda
gasped and looked at Mick in desperation. "What's my
line? It's gone completely out of my head."

Mick said without hesitation, "Here is your tea,
miss."

"Oh, thanks." She breathed a deep sigh of relief and
repeated the line a few times to herself under her
breath, just to make sure she had it down. Then she

stood up and paced back and forth in front of the prop table. "I don't know what's happening to me. I feel like I'm going to walk out there and have a nervous breakdown."

"What are you afraid of?" Mick asked.

"The audience. That they'll hate me."

Mick took her by the elbow and led her to a tiny peephole in the curtain. "Look through there," he instructed. Amanda peered through and realized she could clearly see the people sitting in the first couple of rows.

"What do you see?"

"A fat lady with a blond bun on the top of her head," Amanda replied.

"How *dare* she hate you?" Mick's voice took on a tone of righteous indignation. "She wouldn't be able to get up on this stage and do what you're doing if you paid her a million dollars."

Amanda giggled, and Mick asked, "What else do you see?"

"A man with a moustache checking his watch."

"That weasel! The play's over in forty minutes. What's he got to do that's so important that he has to check his watch?"

"I don't know," Amanda said between giggles, "but now he's yawning."

"That does it!" Mick led her back to the prop table, then grasped her firmly by both shoulders and looked into her eyes. "You get out there and say your line directly to him. Wake him up!"

"Okay!" Amanda saluted with a smile. Mick handed

her the tea tray, and she was amazed to find that nothing was rattling. "Look, Mick! My nerves are gone."

"That's great," Mick replied. "Now go show 'em who's in charge."

"Right!" Amanda moved confidently to where she was to enter.

"Oh, and one more thing," Mick whispered. "Don't try to pick up any of the china. It's all taped to the tray."

Amanda didn't have time to react. Onstage there was an odd silence, and she heard an unfamiliar line coming from Kitty. "Dora? Is that you out there?"

Amanda realized she was supposed to be on the stage. She tried to walk, but her legs seemed paralyzed. Suddenly someone gave her a shove.

"What are you waiting for, babe?" a gruff voice whispered. "Get out there!"

Amanda stumbled onto the stage and was so shocked that she said her line without thinking. "Here is your tea, miss!" She set the tray on the table, and stepped backward to stand by the sideboard.

The action moved just as they'd rehearsed it that afternoon. Kitty tapped Teddy on the shoulder. He spun, clutching the knife in his chest. Then he did a death scene that was twice as long as it had been in rehearsal. He staggered past her and clutched the desk, all the while making horrible rattling sounds in his throat. Then he threw his head back and limped to the couch, collapsing on his back across the cushions with his eyes wide open.

Amanda couldn't take her eyes off his face. She almost laughed out loud at the hamminess of his death, but quickly covered her face with her hands and pretended to be horrified.

Richard ran on, and Kitty reached for the gun. The stage was suddenly filled with an eerie mist. At the top of the stairs, Jaqueline appeared in her ghostly mask. "Eloise, you must pay for your sins!"

Kitty raised the gun and fired. The explosion rocked the theatre.

At that moment, the whole world seemed to go into slow motion. In the script Kitty was supposed to turn, face the audience, and deliver her big speech. But she just stood there, staring at the smoking gun. Instead of disappearing back into the fog, Jaqueline Cantwell staggered down the stairs. Kitty backed away from her in horror. At first Amanda thought that they had decided to improvise a new ending to the scene.

Then Jaqueline lurched forward and clutched the red velvet curtain. She spun around, and for the first time Amanda saw the blood. Bright crimson streaks stained the front of her white costume.

"You've murdered me!" Jaqueline wailed, pointing her finger at Kitty. Then she slid to the floor.

Kitty dropped the gun and screamed. Skitch raced onto the stage and knelt beside the fallen actress. The audience remained silent, not sure if what they were seeing was part of the play or real. Then Skitch yelled, "Is there a doctor in the audience?"

The uproar was deafening as everyone realized at once that the star of *Murder at Midnight* had just been shot.

CHAPTER TEN

On Saturday morning, Amanda sipped a cup of coffee in the Pickering kitchen and studied the morning headlines. Stories about the shooting incident dominated the front page of the *Chronicle*. Somehow a real bullet had been put in the gun, and Jaqueline Cantwell had been wounded.

The phone hadn't stopped ringing from the moment she got up. Friends from school kept calling to see if Amanda was okay. More than one had wondered if Kitty had shot the actress on purpose.

"Lucky for Kitty that bullet only got Jaqueline in the arm," Amanda murmured to herself. "Otherwise she'd find herself cast in the role of a murderess."

Amanda stirred her coffee and shook her head. *How could we have been so wrong?* she thought. They all had assumed Jaqueline was behind the accidents, and had even been comforted by the thought that each one had been staged just for publicity's sake. But now . . .

Amanda set her coffee down and sighed heavily. Now a potential murderer was on the loose, and she had no idea who it was. She unwrapped a paper napkin and stared at the soggy pastry inside. It was a leftover from the opening night party at the theatre. Pepper had put some of them in her purse before they went home. Although no one had felt like celebrating, the party had been held as planned. The other producers figured it was a shame to let the catered food go to waste.

"This is like a funeral," Pepper had observed, stuffing a pastry filled with shrimp in her mouth, "only no one died."

People from the cast and crew had gathered around the food tables set up in the lobby, talking quietly in little groups. No one looked happy. Amanda had searched the crowd for a sight of Mick, but he was nowhere to be found.

Shortly after the reception had begun, Skitch made a brief announcement to the cast. She hadn't had time to change her clothes, and there were dried bloodstains on her shirt.

"First of all," Skitch began, "the producers have decided that *Murder at Midnight* will continue to run as planned. Maggie Carr will take over Miss Cantwell's part until further notice."

"You mean the show will go on?" Pepper asked incredulously.

"Of course," Teddy muttered as he stocked his plate with several cream puffs. "Tonight's audience will have to come back to see how it ended. This will sell more tickets than anything." He popped a pastry in his mouth and mumbled, "It's a heartless business."

"I was hoping this was my opening and closing night," Amanda said as she sipped her punch. "But it looks like I'm going to be in this play a few more days."

Pepper nodded. "Until they can replace the director. Then they can replace you, and I can give up my not-so-promising career as a dresser."

Shortly afterward, Skitch had ushered everyone into a room where several police officers took their statements. After the police were finished the party broke up. What had started out as a night to remember had turned into one everybody wanted to forget.

As Amanda got up to pour herself another cup of coffee, the phone rang again. It was Miss Wilson, the headmistress at Sutter Academy.

"I was in the audience last night, and I have never been so shocked in my life," the woman said. "Of course, we're all behind Kitty one hundred percent."

"Kitty?" Amanda set the coffeepot down with a clunk. "They don't really suspect her, do they?"

"Well, I'm sorry to say they do. I mean, two thousand people saw her pull the trigger last night."

"But, Miss Wilson," Amanda protested, "Kitty

didn't put the bullet in that gun. Someone else must have."

"That's what I told the police. Simple common sense."

"Police!" Amanda nearly choked. "They called you?"

"Yes, and several of Kitty's classmates. What a horrible situation! Amanda, please be careful."

Amanda said good-bye to Miss Wilson and slumped down in the kitchen chair. Someone was trying to frame Kitty, and she had to stop it. Without hesitation Amanda picked up the phone again and dialed.

"Fleet Street," a voice answered on the other end of the line.

"Mick? This is Amanda."

"Mandy. You okay?"

"I'm fine." Amanda couldn't help smiling at the concern in his voice. "But Kitty's not. The police actually think she put the bullet in the gun."

"That's probably 'cause some clown told them she wanted Miss Cantwell dead."

Amanda gasped. "But that was in rehearsal, and she was just upset."

Mick sighed. "Threats don't go over big with the cops."

"Well, we've got to do something about it."

"Like what?"

"Like find out who put the bullet in the gun."

"And how do we do that?"

"We find out who Jaqueline's enemies are."

"Okay, Miss Hart, sounds like you've got a plan."

"I do. Are you game?"

"Lay it on me."

By one P.M. Mick and Amanda were tiptoeing down the halls of Bay General Hospital. Amanda clutched her leather notebook in her hand. Mick had a spiral notepad stuffed in his coat pocket and Pepper's Nikon camera slung across his shoulder.

"I'm not too sure about this," Mick said, as they rounded the corner by the nurses' station. "Jaqueline Cantwell is like the Dragon Lady. One false move, and we're toast."

"Don't worry," Amanda said, trying to sound confident. "We just have to keep several steps ahead of her."

"You sure she won't recognize us?"

"Positive." Amanda smoothed her hair back with one hand. She was wearing a tailored green linen suit that matched her eyes, and had borrowed her cousin's horn-rimmed glasses just to be on the safe side. They were for reading and magnified everything. "Miss Cantwell never really saw me because Maggie stood in for her at my one rehearsal."

"What about last night?"

"She was shot the moment after she entered. I doubt very much that she was checking out the new girl playing the maid."

"Good." Mick smiled. "I just wanted to be sure. I know she's never seen me. And even if she had, actresses never remember stagehands."

"Then we're safe." Amanda took a deep breath and marched up to the nurse's desk.

A young nurse, who didn't look any older than Amanda, was sitting at the station, filling out medical charts. "May I help you?"

"Yes." Suddenly Amanda panicked. *This dumb charade will never work*, she thought. Her voice was shaking. "I'm Amanda Hart, and this is . . . this is . . ."

"Michael J. Soul." Mick flipped up his collar and stepped forward confidently. "We're here to talk to Miss Cantwell."

"Is she expecting you?" the nurse replied, looking back at her writing. "Official visiting hours are from two to four, if you'd care to wait."

Mick turned to Mandy and said in exasperation, "Didn't Perry say he'd called her?"

Amanda knew Mick was up to something, but she didn't have the faintest idea what. She stammered, "I-I *think* he said he got through this morning."

Mick chuckled and slipped his sunglasses on top of his head. "Perry White's our editor at *Teen Scene*."

The nurse's eyes widened, obviously impressed. "I think I've heard of him."

Amanda fought the urge to giggle. Of course the girl had heard of Perry White. That was the name of Clark Kent's editor in the *Superman* movies.

"Listen, we came out on the red-eye flight from New York last night to cover the big rock benefit at Candlestick Park."

"Really?" The nurse's eyes grew even wider.

"Yeah." Mick pushed back his sleeve and checked his watch casually. "Our editor suggested we interview Miss Cantwell while we're in town."

"Gee, I don't know," the nurse said, biting her lip nervously. "Miss Cantwell's supposed to be resting right now."

Mick stepped over to the window across from the nurses' station and flipped open the venetian blinds. He pointed to Gabe, who was leaning against the door of the black limousine. "Our driver is waiting to take us over to the stadium. We'd only be able to see Miss Cantwell for a few minutes."

"If you're from a magazine, I'm sure Miss Cantwell would want to talk to you." The young woman shrugged helplessly. "But I was told not to let her have any visitors."

Mick held up his hands. "Hey, I don't know if we can wait." Mick looked at Amanda and asked, "What do you think? Do we have the time?"

Amanda shook her head. "I don't know, we do have to talk to Bruce later this afternoon."

"*Springsteen?*" the nurse gasped.

"You're right," Mick agreed. "We'd better go." He flipped his glasses down on his nose and turned to leave.

"Wait!" the nurse called after them. "I guess one little short visit wouldn't hurt."

Mick looked dubious. "We're running pretty tight as it is."

"Oh, listen, please take just a few minutes with

Miss Cantwell," the nurse urged. "I'm sure she'd really appreciate it."

Mick sighed heavily. "Well . . . if you insist. But only five minutes."

"Oh, thank you." The nurse giggled. "And I promise you won't be disturbed." She gestured down the hall. "Room 112."

Mick grinned and said, "I'll tell the boss you said hello."

As they hurried down the corridor, Amanda whispered out of the corner of her mouth, "That was ultra cool. I'm impressed."

"The Dragon Lady is going to be a little harder. We'll need a different approach." He put down his collar, straightened his tie, and then tapped on the door. "Miss Cantwell?"

"I thought I made it quite clear I was *not* to be disturbed," an irritated voice answered from within.

Mick stuck his head in the door and smiled. "Hello, Miss Cantwell, Michael Soultaire. I'm with the *Hollywood Reporter*."

"*Hollywood Reporter?*" She sat straight up in her bed, then looked at him suspiciously. "You're awfully young, aren't you?"

"Youth is a state of mind," Michael replied, flashing his winning smile. "I got a call from my editor this morning. He wants me to do a feature on you for our next issue. I'm only in town for the day, but if it's a bad time . . . well, I'm sure this feature can wait."

"A feature?" Miss Cantwell repeated. "Well . . . maybe I could spare a few moments. Please, come in."

Mick stepped through the door and asked, "Mind if my assistant sits in, too? This is . . . uh, Trixie Hart."

Amanda shot him an irritated look, and mouthed silently, *"Trixie?"*

Mick shrugged helplessly.

"Hart?" Jaqueline narrowed her eyes. "Any relation to Del and Dinah Hart?"

Amanda tensed, thinking her cover was about to be blown. "Yes, they're my parents."

"Oh, come right in, dear. I've admired their work for years."

Mick pulled up a chair next to the actress's bed as Amanda surveyed the room. It was more like a hotel suite, with pretty lace curtains on the windows. Baskets of flowers sat on tables and ledges throughout the room. Amanda wondered who could have sent them, since, as far as she'd seen, Miss Cantwell didn't have any real friends. Several framed photographs sat on her bedside table, along with copies of that morning's newspapers.

"Now, Miss Cantwell," Mick began, "I thought we'd focus more on what lies ahead for you than what's in the past."

"I like that, young man," the actress said. "Most journalists insist on rehashing plays I did thirty—well, many years ago."

Mick took a pencil out of his pocket and a small pad. "Let's begin with that unfortunate accident during the opening of *Murder at Midnight*."

"Oh, please!" Miss Cantwell groaned. "Spare me. I've been talking with detectives all morning."

"I guess I have only one question, really."

"What is it?"

"Do you think it was just an accident?"

Miss Cantwell nervously played with the bandages on her wrist. "I hope it was. But I have no idea how the bullet could have gotten in that pistol. I checked it at intermission."

Amanda spun to look at her. "You did?"

"Of course, dear. These kinds of mishaps are legendary in the theatre. Anytime I have to shoot—or be shot at—I *always* check the gun."

"Then what do you do—after you check the gun?" Amanda inched closer to the foot of Miss Cantwell's bed.

"I return it to Dan Carnegie, my prop man, of course," came the swift reply. "He locks it in the prop cabinet until shortly before it's set on the prop table."

"Could he have put the bullet in the gun?" Mick asked.

"Dan? Never. He's my friend. Been with me for years. Besides," she added sensibly, "he'd be the first one anyone would suspect."

Amanda peered over the top of her glasses and made a note in her book to talk to Dan later.

"But why are we lingering on all of this unpleasantness?" Miss Cantwell complained. "I thought this interview was to focus on my career."

Amanda pointed to the photo on the bedside table and smoothly changed the subject. "Is that your husband, George Cantwell?"

Miss Cantwell's face softened as she picked up the

photo. It was of three people in bathing suits at the ocean. "Yes, that's dear George and me on our first trip to Catalina."

"Who's that with you?" Mick asked, leaning forward. "Looks familiar."

"Teddy Ballard." Jaqueline laughed lightly and tapped the picture frame. "He was *always* with us."

"Oh, was that when you first did *Murder at Midnight*?"

"Good heavens, no!" She laughed. "This trip was years before."

"Old friends, huh," Mick said.

"*Old* is right." As Miss Cantwell reached for her pack of cigarettes, she whispered to Mick, "Don't tell." She lit one and said, "Teddy and I have known each other since we were seventeen."

It was hard for Amanda to imagine Jaqueline and Teddy at that age. She wondered if they'd always been so dramatic, or if they were ever just regular teenagers.

"What about the playwright?" Mick asked. He glanced at his own notepad. "Uh . . . Alfred Crane?"

Miss Cantwell took another puff on her cigarette and leaned back against her pillows. "I met Alfred when he was first trying to be an actor." She giggled and said, "He was almost as bad an actor as he is a playwright." She exhaled a large puff of smoke and added, "But that's strictly off the record, do you understand?"

Mick nodded. "You don't think *Murder at Midnight* is a good play?"

"Now it is," Jaqui declared, "but when Alfred first brought it to us, it was a disaster, just a hangnail of an idea. Dear George worked on it night and day to make it playable. It was only out of the goodness of his heart that he let Alfred keep his name on it."

Amanda wrote Alfred Crane's name in her notebook and underlined it several times. Then Amanda asked, "Miss Cantwell, do you plan to return to *Murder at Midnight*?"

Jaqueline Cantwell looked at her in total amazement. "But, of course, darling. I'm not going to let one tiny accident spoil my comeback."

A light tap sounded on the door, and the young blond nurse stuck her head in. "Excuse me, Miss Cantwell, but these just arrived for you. They're from the theatre."

She held up a large floral wreath, and Jaqueline Cantwell smiled happily. "Ah, they must be from my colleagues in the play. We never forget one another in our times of need."

The gloomy wreath looked like it belonged at a funeral. Amanda pretended to write down Miss Cantwell's words.

"Well, thank you very much for the interview, Miss Cantwell." Mick stood up and said, "We really need to be on our way."

"Must you?" Miss Cantwell looked suddenly forlorn.

Amanda realized they had brought the camera but hadn't used it. "Do you mind if we get one shot of you

before we go? It will look fabulous on the cover of
Teen—"

"*Reporter!*" Mick corrected her quickly. "Yes, the,
um, *Hollywood Reporter*. Why don't we get a picture
of you reading your card from the cast?"

"Wonderful!" Miss Cantwell quickly ran a brush
through her hair and applied some fresh lipstick. Mick
and Amanda waited patiently as she blotted the
lipstick, then lightly powdered her nose. She pushed
the collar of her bed jacket up around her neck with
her good hand. "I'm sorry, dear," she said, still holding
her pose, "would you open the card for me? I seem to
have only one hand available."

"Sure." Amanda slipped the little card out of the
envelope as Mick raised the camera to his eye. "Now,
look at the card and smile."

Miss Cantwell glanced down at the card, and her
face froze in a hideous grimace as the flash went off.
Amanda read the message on the card and gasped.

Don't come back, it read, *or next time the bullet
won't miss*.

CHAPTER ELEVEN

Gabe drove the limousine up to the hospital entrance at breakneck speed. He arrived with a squeal of tires moments after two orderlies deposited Mick and Amanda on the front sidewalk.

Pepper, who'd been sipping a soft drink in the passenger seat beside him, screeched, "Gabe, give me some warning, will you? I am now wearing twelve ounces of cola down the entire front of my vest."

"Sorry, *chica*," Gabe replied, unlocking the back door. "But Mick and Mandy looked like they were in trouble."

The door flew open, and Mick and Amanda slid hurriedly into the rear seat of the limousine. Gabe stepped on the accelerator, and the black car pulled away from the hospital into traffic.

"Wow!" Mick exclaimed. "That was incredible."

"Well, what happened?" Pepper asked, completely forgetting about her soggy clothes.

"She flipped out," Mick said. "The woman went completely over the top."

Amanda shook her head. "I've never seen anything like it. One minute she's cool and collected, and the next she's having a total breakdown."

"It took two nurses to stick her," Mick added.

"Stick her?" Pepper repeated. "She was stabbed?"

"With a needle," Amanda explained. "They gave her a sedative to calm her down."

"Then two thugs in green outfits grabbed us and showed us the door."

"That really makes me mad, too," Amanda said. "I mean, we didn't have anything to do with her attack. It was the note."

Pepper held up one hand. "You lost me. What note?"

"The anonymous one that arrived with some flowers," Mick explained. "Weird flowers, too, like a funeral wreath."

Amanda nodded. "It said that if she came back to the show, the next bullet wouldn't miss."

Gabe shook his head. "Man, that's heavy."

Pepper pushed her glasses up on her nose. "Does she have any idea who sent the note?"

"She doesn't have any idea about anything," Mick said. "She's sawing logs right now, and will probably stay that way till tomorrow."

"So what do we do now?" Gabe asked. "I don't like to drive around in circles."

"I think we should go over the suspects carefully," Amanda said, reaching into her purse for a notepad, "and get to the bottom of this, once and for all—"

"Whoa," Mick cut in. "I can't think on an empty stomach."

"Now that you mention it," Pepper said, "I'm starved. I haven't eaten a thing except shrimp-and-cheese puffs since last night."

"Yo, Gabe!" Mick leaned forward and rested his elbows on the back of the driver's seat. "What say we treat the girls to dinner?"

"Outstanding." Gabe grinned at him in the mirror. "I know the perfect place."

Amanda and Pepper exchanged interested glances. Here they were, in a sleek, luxurious limousine. The boys would probably take them to a place with valet parking. Pepper sat up suddenly. "Wait a minute, we're not really dressed right."

"Hey, it's cool," Mick replied, flipping his glasses down onto his nose. "We know the maître d'."

Fifteen minutes later, Gabe slowed the car to a stop in front of the seediest diner Amanda had ever seen. It was the old-fashioned kind that looked like a train, or a trailer. At one time the exterior had been diagonal stripes of silver with blue metallic trim, but rust and the weather had taken their toll. Now Amanda could barely make out the neon sign that read "Al's Place."

"What is this, a joke?" Pepper demanded, peering through the windshield of the limousine.

"Al's is no joke," Mick said. "People come from all over the city to eat here."

"What attracts them," Pepper grumbled as she got out of the car, "the view?" She pointed to the abandoned brick building across the street from the diner. Next to it lay a vacant lot surrounded by a chain-link fence topped with barbed wire.

"Naw, the food." Mick held open the glass door of the diner as the girls stepped through the weathered entrance. "Al's has the best chili dogs and buffalo burgers in the city."

"Buffalo burgers?" Pepper froze in her tracks. "Did he say buffalo burgers?"

"I believe so." Amanda couldn't help giggling. The freckled redhead had turned absolutely green.

"I'll just have a rye crisp and a glass of water," Pepper croaked.

"This is like walking into a time warp," Amanda said, looking around the interior of the diner. "Instant fifties."

A curved formica counter ran the length of the tiny room. About half a dozen circular aluminum stools with red vinyl seats were screwed to the linoleum-tiled floor. A thin old man with a bristly crew cut and a white apron stuck his head through an opening in the wall behind the counter. His wrinkled face burst into a smile.

"Al, my man!" Mick called out.

"Mickey! Gabe! You boys are a sight for sore eyes. Pull up a chair, and I'll be right with you." He pulled his head back into the steam-filled kitchen and shouted, "Break's over. We got customers."

Mick and Gabe led them to a table by the window, and Al brought them glasses of water and menus. Amanda and Pepper were relieved to see that the diner had more to offer than buffalo burgers. The gang ordered quickly, and Al shuffled off to the kitchen. Then Amanda dug into her purse and pulled out her leather-bound notebook.

"Okay," she said, "let's get down to business. Two questions: *who* tried to kill Jaqueline Cantwell, and *how* did they get the bullet in the gun?"

Pepper spoke up first. "I think it has to be Alfred Crane. Did you see the look on his face when he found out that Miss Cantwell had kept his play from being done for ten years?"

Amanda nodded. "I'd probably feel like strangling her myself if I were him. Even if Jaqueline did say that her husband wrote the play." She put Alfred Crane at the top of the list.

Mick shook his head. "I say Richard Tyson is the big contender."

"No kiddin', man," Gabe agreed. "That dude is holding a major grudge against Jaqueline Cantwell. That's all he talks about in the limo."

"And now that she's out of the picture," Amanda observed, "he'll probably get that top billing he wanted."

"What about Maggie Carr?" Pepper suggested. "She sure has a lot to gain by Jaqueline's early demise."

"That's true," Amanda said, printing Maggie's name

below Richard's. "And from the way she acted yesterday, there's a real volcano brewing inside her."

Gabe took a sip of his water, then asked, "What about that director guy?"

"Cliff Verdery? Naw." Mick waved the suggestion away with his hand. "That joker wasn't even there last night."

"Wait a minute!" Amanda sat bolt upright in her chair. "He was too! I caught sight of him just as I was going onstage. In fact, he shoved me when I was late for my entrance."

"What?" Pepper exclaimed. "Why didn't you say something?"

"It completely slipped my mind," Amanda replied, "what with all the commotion right afterward."

"Well, I'd move Cliff Verdery to the top of the list," Pepper declared.

"Yeah, the guy certainly has a motive," Mick added. "I mean, Miss C. gave him the heave-ho right in front of the entire cast and crew. Pretty humiliating."

"And don't forget," Amanda said, "this production was supposed to be his ticket to Broadway. Getting fired from the show took that away from him."

"What about Teddy Ballard and Dan Carnegie?" Pepper asked. "Those guys have known her for years."

Amanda chewed thoughtfully on the end of her pen. "I've thought about them, but where's the motive? Okay, so Teddy hates his part in the show, but enough to try and kill someone? I don't know. And as for Dan . . ."

"Nothing," Mick said. "Except that, as the prop

master, he could have put that bullet in the gun easier than anyone else." Mick shook his head. "But I just don't see him doing something like that."

A loud thunk on the swinging door signaled Al's return. "Dinner is served. Here you go, boys—two buffalo burgers, with everything on 'em, and Texas fries. And for you gals—Al's Chef Salad Supreme."

As Al set her plate in front of her, Amanda realized that she was starved. All four of them dug into their food with a vengeance.

"Hey, this dressing is great," Amanda said, crunching on her lettuce.

"Of course," Mick replied with a grin. "Would we steer you wrong?"

"There is one person that we haven't mentioned," Pepper said, reaching for one of Gabe's Texas fries, which were French fries covered with melted cheese and jalapeño peppers. She popped it in her mouth and mumbled, "Kitty."

Amanda nearly choked on a tomato slice. "Pepper! How can you even say that? Kitty's our friend."

"She's also an actress who hates Jaqueline Cantwell."

"Enough to kill her?" Amanda shook her head. "Not in a million years."

Pepper shrugged. "All of this publicity could be a big boost to her career. Right now everyone's feeling sorry for her 'cause she was framed. Her name's on the front page of every newspaper in the Bay Area."

Amanda set her fork down with a clang. "Okay, I'll admit that Kitty is really driven about her career. But she's not stupid enough to risk spending a lifetime behind bars just to get her name in the paper."

"This is really confusing," Pepper said, taking another of Gabe's fries. "It seems like practically everyone involved had a reason to get rid of Jaqueline Cantwell."

"Which is why we should trust no one," Amanda said.

"Including Kitty," Pepper said stubbornly.

Mick studied Amanda's list of suspects for a few minutes while everyone ate hungrily. Then he said, "I think we could narrow this down if we figured out who had access to the prop table after Dan checked the gun for the final time."

"That backstage is a maze," Pepper said. "People seem to come in and out from everywhere."

"Which is why we should check it out carefully," Mick replied. "It's not as complicated as it looks."

"Great idea." Amanda put her napkin on her plate and stood up. "Let's go."

"What about dessert?" Gabe protested.

"You just devoured an entire buffalo, and a double order of fries." Pepper gaped at him in amazement. "How can you even *think* of putting more food inside you?"

Mick punched Gabe on the shoulder. "She's right. We'd better go. We've got a murder to solve."

"But no one's been murdered," Pepper corrected him.

"Not yet."

Mick's words hung in the air like an ominous warning.

Less than half an hour later, Amanda and Mick stepped onto the empty stage of the Gateway Theatre. The auditorium was completely dark, and the solitary lamp known as the safety light stood in the middle of the stage, casting eerie shadows against the floor and walls of the set.

Gabe had dropped them off early and then gone to pick up Richard Tyson. Pepper was needed in the wardrobe department for costume repairs, so it was left to Amanda and Mick to reconstruct the scene of the crime. The stage was exactly the way it had been when Jaqueline Cantwell had been shot the night before.

"Without the lights and people, this place is really creepy," Amanda whispered.

"Yeah," Mick answered in a low voice. "It makes you believe in those stories about theatre ghosts."

"Ghosts? Here at the Gateway?" Amanda could feel her heart pounding. She instinctively moved closer to Mick. Just as her pulse started to quiet, another sound sent it racing again.

"Do you hear that?" She could barely move her lips.

Mick nodded. "Footsteps." He grabbed her arm and led her to the little alcove under the staircase. "Let's duck in here."

The two of them crouched in the shadows of the stairwell. Soon, a familiar figure in coveralls appeared. Amanda exhaled a shaky breath of relief as she watched Dan Carnegie move about the set, placing new candles in the candle holders after removing the old ones. He set out a fresh box of matches on the sideboard. After each task he'd make a check mark on the clipboard he carried under his arm. Finally he picked up the tea set that Amanda had carried on the night before and returned it to the prop table backstage.

"Thank goodness it was just—" Amanda's words were cut off as Mick clamped one hand over her mouth. He pointed to the shadows by the wings. Someone was moving carefully across the stage. The floor squeaked and the person froze, silhouetted against the single bulb of the safety light. Amanda couldn't see his face, but she recognized what he clutched in his hands. It was a crowbar.

The figure inched along the outer walls toward the set piece holding the French doors. He knelt down and Amanda heard a soft groan from the floor, as if a board were being pried apart. Amanda nearly gasped as she realized he was trying to wreck the set.

Suddenly, the lobby doors burst open and the voices of the housekeeping staff and the sound of a vacuum cleaner could be heard. The figure dropped the crowbar behind the sideboard and scurried off the stage. As he passed the safety light, Amanda got a good look at his face. She dug her nails into Mick's arm as she hissed, "It's Alfred Crane, the playwright!"

CHAPTER TWELVE

Amanda sat in shock as she watched Mick quickly nail the wall supports to the floor. "What should we do?" she asked. "Call the police?"

"And tell 'e᷈ that we saw Alfred Crane with a crowbar on the s᷈ t of his own play?" Mick shook his head. "They'll say he was just trying to fix the wall. Besides, no one got hurt, so no crime was committed."

"I don't get it," Amanda said. "Why would he try to hurt the cast?"

"I'm not sure he was trying to do that. Take a look at this."

Amanda stood up and peered at the boards along the bottom of the set piece. "I'm sorry, I don't get it."

"This wall is rigged to fall over backward. It would

have hit the wall of the building and made a loud noise, but that's all."

"Well, it certainly would have stopped the show."

Footsteps sounded behind them, and Amanda half-expected to see Alfred Crane wielding something more menacing, like an ax. But it was only Dan Carnegie.

"Mick, I'm glad you're here early." Dan was carrying a wooden box under one arm. "We've got to tighten security on everything that goes on and off that stage. I've put extra lights by the prop table, and the management's assigned us a security guard who'll be backstage at all times."

Mick gestured to Amanda. "Dan, you know Mandy Hart. She's in the play."

"Pleased to meet you." Dan smiled, and his face creased into hundreds of little wrinkles. "You're the replacement for that poor kid Sally Quince, aren't you?"

"That's right," Amanda replied.

"Everything's been so haywire in the last few days, I haven't had a chance to keep up with all the changes being made in the show."

"Oh, Amanda, there you are!"

Amanda turned to see Kitty standing behind them on the stage. She stood near the single bulb of the safety light. The stark contrast of the light against her profile reminded Amanda of that first night when Kitty had posed beneath the stage door lamp. She looked paler now, much more the frightened teenager than the sophisticated young actress.

"Are you okay, Kitty?" Amanda went and hugged her friend warmly. "I know you must have had an awful time of it."

Kitty nodded. "The police talked to me for hours last night. Then today they were all over my house, poking into everything. They've even stationed this awful Detective Wick in the green room. He says it's to protect us, but I think he's spying on me." She shivered. "It gives me the creeps!"

"What do they want to know?" Mick asked, coming up beside them.

"Who put the real bullet in the gun," Kitty replied, turning to focus her clear blue eyes on Mick.

"Seems like that's the question on everyone's lips," Mick observed.

Kitty lay her hand on Dan Carnegie's arm and asked, "Dan, is there any way something could have happened *after* I handed you the gun?"

Dan shook his head slowly. "After you checked it, I checked it. Then I handed it straight over to Richard Tyson."

"Richard Tyson?" Amanda repeated.

"That's right," Kitty said. "He brings the pistol onstage and places it on the table."

"And he barely has time to change his jacket, comb his hair, get the pistol, and go back onstage," Dan added. "Less than fifteen seconds."

"Well, it's all very upsetting," Kitty declared, her chin starting to quiver. "I don't know how I'll be able to shoot that gun again tonight."

Amanda placed a sympathetic arm around her

friend's shoulder. "Maybe you should have your understudy go on for you tonight."

Kitty's eyes widened in horror. "Are you out of your mind? More important people are going to be here tonight than were here for opening."

Amanda was taken aback at the force of her reaction. "I just thought that, if you were so upset . . ."

"I'll be fine, don't worry." Kitty wiped a tear away from her eye and tilted her chin up bravely. Amanda remembered how Kitty had struck just that pose for her big speech the first night Amanda had seen the play. "I . . . I just want to know for sure that it will never happen again," Kitty said.

Dan patted her arm. "Don't you worry, honey." He held up the wooden box under his arm. "I'm locking this gun in a safe until just before it's needed. And a security guard will be watching the entire show."

"Before you put it away in the safe," Kitty said, "I'd like to check it myself. Just so I'll feel better."

"Sure." Dan set the box down on the stage and opened it. Inside lay a gleaming silver pistol resting on a cushion of green velvet. There was an identical slot for another gun. Amanda reasoned that the missing pistol was the one used in the shooting and had been taken by the police as evidence.

Kitty picked up the gun, released the ammunition clip, checked the chamber, slid the clip back into the handle, then set the pistol back into the case.

Amanda watched, dumbfounded. Finally she said, "Boy, Kitty, you handle that thing like a pro."

Kitty smiled. "When I found out I'd have to shoot a

gun in the show, I signed up for some lessons at a shooting range in Oakland."

Mick had been leaning against the brick wall of backstage, watching silently. Suddenly he said, "Do that again."

Kitty looked startled. "Do what?"

"Take out the clip and put it back in again."

Kitty looked confused for a moment. Then she glared at Mick. "What for? To show that I'm guilty, or something?"

"No, no." Mick smiled his slow, sexy smile that Amanda knew could melt a girl's heart. "I just want to see how long it takes to do the whole thing."

"Well . . . okay." Kitty sounded unconvinced. "But just once."

"Time her, Mandy," Mick said. Amanda checked her wristwatch as Kitty ran through the procedure again.

"Five seconds," Amanda announced. "Hardly any time at all. That means if Dan turned his head away to check another prop, or something, anyone could have had time to change the clip on the pistol."

"Do you remember doing anything like that?" Mick asked the prop master. "Any unusual distractions?"

"I don't think so." Dan scratched his head. "To tell you the truth, I can't be absolutely positive." His weathered face suddenly looked very tired.

Mick patted the old man's shoulder gently. "Don't sweat it, Dan. Miss Cantwell wasn't seriously hurt, and tonight you've got that guard with you."

Dan nodded wearily. He tucked the pistol box under his arm and shuffled off into the darkness.

"Mick, you are so clever!" Kitty said, her voice full of relief. "Thank you for noticing that about the pistol." She flashed her practiced smile at Mick and then hugged Amanda. "I knew having you here would be good for me."

Amanda watched Kitty disappear off down the stairs. A tiny seed of doubt was beginning to grow inside her. Kitty was awfully good with that pistol, almost too good. Right after the shooting incident, she had seemed genuinely upset, and had even cried. But she was an actress and could do that at the drop of a hat. Amanda shook her head to clear it. *She's your friend,* she scolded herself silently. *You've got to trust that.*

Mick waved one hand in front of Amanda's face. "Uh, Mandy. Anybody home?"

Amanda blinked. Mick was standing very close to her, looking into her face with his piercing blue eyes. The darkness felt like a cloak around them.

"What?"

"I was just saying," he repeated with a grin, "maybe you should go downstairs, since it's getting close to half hour."

"I guess you're right. I'd better go." Reluctantly she stepped away.

"In the meantime, I'll keep my eyes peeled, in case Alfred Crane decides to do any more remodeling on his set."

Amanda said good-bye and quickly made her way down through the tunnel into the green room. A man in a dark blue blazer and a grumpy expression was leaning against the far wall by the call board where rehearsals were posted. He looked her over suspiciously as she came in. *That must be Detective Wick*, Amanda thought.

Richard Tyson was already in costume and seated on the couch, talking with Teddy Ballard and Alfred Crane.

"We're sold out for the next two months!" the playwright was saying gleefully. "People *want* to see this play. We're a hit!"

"Oh, Alfred, calm down," Richard said sourly. "It's just morbid curiosity that's selling tickets. People want to see us drop dead."

Teddy nodded. "They're all ghouls."

Their comments sent the playwright off into a rambling, incoherent defense of his play, which the other two actors pointedly ignored. Then Pepper's familiar red head popped out of one of the dressing rooms.

"Pssst! Amanda!"

"What is it?" Amanda called back loudly.

Pepper gave her an exasperated look and said, "Come here. It's an ecret-say."

"Ecret-say?" Amanda repeated. Then it hit her. "Secret." She scurried over to the door. Pepper grabbed her by the wrist and pulled her into the dressing room. She shut and locked the door behind them.

"Some detective you are!" she said. "Don't you know a code when you hear one?"

"Using pig latin as a secret code went out in the third grade," Amanda protested.

"It's the only thing I could think of at the moment." Then Pepper lowered her voice. "We don't have much time. Look what I found on the floor beside Maggie Carr's dressing table."

She held up a small yellow notepad. Scribbled on it were some words and a phone number.

"Cable Car Florists," Amanda read out loud. "What's that got to do with anything?"

Pepper exhaled a breath of air that sent her bangs fluttering. "Look at what's written below it."

"Bay General Hospital." Amanda's eyes widened, and she immediately dropped her voice to an urgent whisper. "You don't think it was Maggie who sent that wreath, do you?"

"I can't see her sending a get-well bouquet of flowers," Pepper said. "Certainly not after what she said about Jaqueline at the rehearsal."

"Maggie certainly has the most to gain by Jaqueline Cantwell's not coming back to the show." Amanda sank down in the dressing chair. "But if she sent the flowers—did she try to *kill* Jaqueline?"

"What are you girls doing in here?"

Amanda sprang to her feet. She couldn't believe her eyes. It looked like Jaqueline Cantwell standing in the doorway. Then she realized that it was Maggie Carr, dressed in Jaqueline's costume and wig.

"I'm sorry, Miss Carr," Pepper said, blushing hotly. "I was just cleaning up and I found this." She held up the yellow slip of paper.

Maggie's eye twitched. "What's that?"

"You know what it is," Amanda said, studying her face intently. "You sent that threatening note to Miss Cantwell at the hospital, didn't you?"

Maggie met her gaze steadily. After what seemed like an eternity, she answered in an icy voice, "Yes. I did."

"But why?"

The actress turned to check her makeup in the mirror. "Opportunity knocked, and I answered." Maggie carefully licked a finger and smoothed her eyebrow. "The longer she stays in the hospital, the longer I play the part."

"A death threat is very serious, Miss Carr," Amanda warned.

"So is attempted murder," a voice behind them declared. It was Detective Wick. He slouched in the doorway with his hands in the pockets of his wrinkled brown suit. "I overheard everything."

"B-but . . ." Maggie stammered. "I didn't mean . . ."

"I have to take you in for questioning," the detective said.

Maggie sagged against the wall and put her head in her hands.

"Places, everyone," Skitch's voice said over the loudspeaker. The announcement seemed to give Maggie new resolve.

"I'm sorry, officer, you'll have to wait." The actress assumed a regal posture. "Two thousand people are waiting for my performance this evening, and I'm not going to disappoint them."

"Maggie Carr, to the stage, please!" Skitch ordered over the intercom. The policeman hesitated for a moment, unsure of what to do.

"Detective Wick, please let her do the show," Amanda said quietly. "She's waited her whole life for this moment. She won't run away."

"Places, *please!*" the loudspeaker crackled.

Finally the detective nodded. "But I'll be watching you." Amanda and Pepper watched as he looped his arm in Maggie's and escorted her to the stage.

CHAPTER THIRTEEN

I t's simply tragic about Maggie Carr," Teddy Ballard declared later that night after the play.

Detective Wick had taken the actress into custody right after the curtain call. She'd been whisked off to the police station without even being allowed to say good-bye. Amanda and Pepper had joined the other cast members at the Curtain Up restaurant, across the street from the theatre. Mick had stayed behind to pack up the props with Dan Carnegie.

"I feel bad for Maggie," Pepper whispered to Amanda, "but at least that puts Kitty in the clear."

Amanda crossed her fingers. "I hope."

"Who would have thought Maggie had it in her?" Teddy mused. "It must be dreadful for her in that cell."

"They haven't arrested her," Amanda said, taking a sip of her cola. "They've just taken her in for questioning."

Richard Tyson, who had gotten a drink at the bar, pulled up a chair to their table. "Well, I'm just glad they gave her a chance to do the show at least once."

"And she was brilliant, wasn't she?" a familiar voice declared from the front of the tiny restaurant.

"Cliff!" Teddy greeted their former director with his arms spread wide. "It's good to see you. Were you at the show tonight?"

"Of course I was there," Cliff said, as he sat down beside Amanda. "I worked with Maggie all day on the role."

The memory of him lurking backstage moments before Jaqueline had been shot the night before made Amanda feel distinctly uncomfortable to be near him. A sudden thought crossed her mind: *Could Cliff and Maggie have planned the note—and the accidents—together?*

"Well, the work showed. She was marvelous tonight." Richard raised his glass as a toast. "Congratulations."

"Thank you." Cliff bowed his head. "Or, more precisely, thanks to Maggie Carr."

"Hear, hear!" Teddy echoed.

Their waitress arrived with a plate of hot nachos for the group, and a shrimp cocktail for Teddy. He took a forkful and turned to Cliff. "I suppose you heard that the police have taken Maggie in to talk about the shooting and all of that."

"Yes," Cliff snapped. "And I think it's absurd. Maggie would never try to kill anyone."

Richard Tyson shrugged. "She admitted sending that wreath and the threatening note."

"That was just a ploy to keep Jaqueline away from the show." Cliff took a sip of his drink and chuckled. "Pretty neat trick. I wish I'd thought of it weeks ago. We'd have had considerably smoother sailing."

A burst of laughter at the next table made Amanda turn in her chair. Nearby, Alfred Crane was regaling a few of the actors from the party scene with a theatre story.

"Look at him," Pepper whispered. "He's on cloud nine."

Amanda nodded. "Every gruesome thing that happens to this play just makes him happier and happier."

They exchanged quick looks, and Pepper muttered under her breath, "*Très* weird."

Meanwhile, Richard was saying, "I can understand why Maggie would send the note and wreath, but how did she get the bullet in the pistol?"

Teddy took another bite of shrimp. "You've got me there."

"She says she stayed in her dressing room the entire play," Amanda stated, "except for when she had to be onstage."

"I know she did," Pepper said, "because I talked to her several times there."

"And even if she did somehow manage to sneak out of her dressing room and put the bullet in the gun," Richard asked, "why would she rig the stairs?"

"To throw suspicion away from herself," Amanda offered.

"But Maggie is the one who took that fall," Cliff interjected. "She could have been seriously hurt."

"Not if she'd practiced," Amanda said. "Most actors know how to take a fall safely."

Teddy finished his shrimp and wiped his mouth. "My, my. You all sound like amateur detectives."

Richard reached for a nacho. "We're just trying to get to the bottom of this mess. It's entirely possible that more than one person is behind these so-called accidents."

A nervous murmur went around the table. Amanda glanced over at Alfred Crane. She and Mick had watched him deliberately try to damage the set. What else might he have done?

"Speaking of detectives," Pepper declared, "Amanda's pretty good at solving mysteries."

Amanda kicked Pepper under the table. Pepper shot her a pained look but continued. "At Sutter Academy she uncovered a criminal ring and unmasked the leader.

"Really?" Teddy asked, arching his white eyebrows curiously.

Amanda glared at Pepper, trying to reach her with mental telepathy to get her to shut up. Pepper rambled on, "Of course she gets it from her parents, who are terrific journalists—"

"Try this, Pepper, it's great." Amanda shoved a nacho in her friend's mouth. Then she smiled sweetly at the others. "Pepper exaggerates—a lot."

Richard Tyson leaned forward. "Assuming you do have a talent for detection, what would be your first move in investigating this case?"

Amanda could tell by his tone that he was just humoring her. She bit back a smart reply and answered simply, "Find out who wants Jaqueline out of the show."

Cliff Verdery and Richard Tyson looked at each other, and chorused, "Everyone."

"Now, dears, be kind," Teddy said. "After all, Jaqui is the one who hired us—"

"And fired us," Cliff Verdery said bitterly.

"Well, she is in the hospital. You should try to show some sympathy for her." Teddy got up from the table and headed toward the bar in the next room to order another drink.

"Would she show any sympathy for us?" Cliff called after him. "No." He turned back to the others. "Let's face it, she doesn't have any friends."

"You can say that again," Alfred Crane said, as he came up to their table.

"What about Teddy?" Richard objected. "Isn't he her friend?"

"Teddy's another matter," Alfred replied with a shrug. "They go so far back, it's almost beyond friendship. They were engaged to be married once."

"Really?" Amanda gasped. She looked over at the portly, red-faced actor leaning against the bar. It was hard to think of him and Jaqueline being in love.

"Oh, yes," Alfred said after a moment. "It was right out of college. They were engaged for almost a year."

"True, Alfred, so very true." Teddy had rejoined them so quietly that Amanda was startled. For a second she felt embarrassed to be caught talking about his personal life, but he didn't seem to mind. "Mercifully, Jaqui and I discovered we were much better off as friends. If we'd gotten married, it would have been too, too terrible."

"Was she always like this?" Amanda asked.

"Like what, my dear?" Teddy gave her a pleasant smile.

"You know, so dramatic and . . . well, nasty."

Teddy threw back his head and laughed. "She was even worse. You might say she's mellowed with age."

Cliff took a sip of his drink and muttered, "If that's mellow, then I'm a monkey's uncle."

"Well, at least we don't have to put up with her anymore," Alfred Crane said cheerily. "She's safely away in the hospital. The play can run smoothly and be a big hit."

"With what actress in the lead?" Teddy demanded.

"Why, Maggie, of cour—" Alfred's hand flew to his mouth. "Oh, dear, I forgot they've taken her to jail. Who's going to play Jaqui's part now?"

Just then Skitch, looking more haggard than ever, came into the restaurant and slumped in the chair next to Cliff. "You'll never believe who I just talked to on the phone."

"Who?" the entire group asked in unison.

"Jacqueline Cantwell. She heard about Maggie's arrest, and she's decided to return to the play."

Six faces stared at her in stunned silence.

CHAPTER FOURTEEN

Amanda went to the theatre the next night with the most awful sinking feeling inside of her. To make matters worse, a big storm had swept in from the bay, and her coat was soaked with rain. From the moment she opened the stage door, Amanda knew something was wrong. The backstage area was deserted. She found the cast and crew down in the green room, all talking at once. As she wove her way through the crowd to her dressing room, Pepper came up beside her.

"The police released Maggie Carr," Pepper hissed.

"Why?"

"They didn't have any proof she put that bullet in the gun."

"But what about the threatening note?" Amanda

asked as they stepped into her dressing room. She hurriedly removed her clothes to change into her costume. "She confessed to sending that."

Pepper shrugged. "They said that's all it was—a threat."

"What time did they release her?" Amanda slipped her maid's black dress over her head.

"About an hour ago," Pepper replied, zipping up the back of her costume. "Skitch has been trying to reach Jaqueline Cantwell at her hotel, but so far, no luck."

Pepper was interrupted by Skitch's voice outside in the hall. "Yes, Maggie's here!"

Amanda stuck her head out the door and saw the stage manager talking to Richard Tyson. "Maggie's in the theatre?" he gasped. "Where?"

"In her dressing room." Skitch pointed to the closed door. "She said she had a show to do, and then disappeared."

"Shouldn't somebody tell her to leave?" Teddy asked, joining the conversation.

Skitch threw up her arms. "Who? Our director has been fired, I can't reach the other producers, and Jaqueline is in transit." Then Skitch shouted to the room in general, "And you know what? I don't really care!"

"I don't want to be around when Jaqueline discovers that Maggie's here," Richard groaned.

"I do," Teddy said, smiling wickedly. "No one throws a scene better than Jaqui. This one should be spectacular."

"Why should we tell her?" Alfred Crane said, twisting his hands nervously. "If Maggie just stays in her dressing room, Jaqui won't know she's here until it's too late. Then the play can continue."

"Dresser!" a voice shouted from one of the dressing rooms.

Pepper groaned, "That's me. Listen, Amanda, this is my last night. I don't care if these people have to go onstage naked, I'm quitting."

Amanda nodded. "I'm with you."

"Dresser!" the voice shouted again.

"Cool your jets, I'm coming!" Pepper bellowed back, then turned to Amanda. "Check you later."

Amanda's head was starting to throb, and she spun in a circle looking for a place to sit down.

"Are you lost, little girl?" a husky voice whispered in her ear.

"Mick!" she gasped, turning around. "You should warn people when you sneak up on them."

"Then that wouldn't be very sneaky, would it?" Mick grinned.

At that moment, Jaqueline Cantwell appeared at the door. The entire green room went quiet as Skitch ran to meet her. Amanda whispered to Mick, "She doesn't know about Maggie yet."

"*What!*" Jaqueline's voice boomed around the room. "This is intolerable. I want her out, and I want her out *now!*"

Jaqueline swept across the green room with her eye firmly fixed on Maggie's dressing room door.

"Mick, let's get out of here," Amanda hissed. "This next part could be really ugly."

"I know just the place." Mick grabbed her by the elbow and led her toward the tunnel that crossed under the stage. "Besides, Dan Carnegie has a theory that I want you to hear. Come on, he's waiting for us."

The tunnel was dark, and she stumbled blindly behind Mick as they crept down the narrow corridor. Halfway down Mick stopped and opened a small white door, stepped over the raised sill and motioned her to come inside.

Amanda remembered the little door from her first time in the theatre. It was hard to believe that was only three days ago.

"This is where the orchestra sits, right?" Her eyes could make out several chairs and music stands in the dim half-light.

"You got it. This is the pit," Mick said with a chuckle.

A man stood up in the corner, and Amanda leaped backward, stifling a scream.

Mick put his hand on her arm. "Relax, it's just Dan."

Amanda tried to relax, but the knot in her stomach was tight. Mick took her hand. "You're awfully jumpy tonight."

"Isn't everyone?" Amanda asked. "I mean, we have a murderer wandering around scot-free, and they're still planning to do this dumb play. I don't get it."

"Nothing makes sense in show biz," Dan said. "I

guess they all think this murder business will sell more tickets. It's what they call good box office."

"Well, I don't see anything good about it." Amanda draped her apron and lace cap over a nearby music stand.

Dan patted one of the metal chairs. "You two have a seat. I've got only a few minutes."

Mick pulled up a chair next to Amanda, and Dan sat across from them. He folded his hands in front of him and said, "See, I've gone over and over the sequence of events the night Jaqueline was shot, and I've come to a conclusion."

"You know who put the bullets in the pistol?" Amanda asked eagerly.

Dan shook his head. "But I think I know how they did it."

"Mick leaned forward in his seat. "Tell her, Dan."

"Onstage. That's the only way."

Amanda cocked her head. "You mean, during a performance, in front of an audience?"

"I think it happened during the blackout in the second act."

Mick nodded. "Richard Tyson brings on the pistol and sets it on the table, he and Jaqueline have a big fight, and then there's a blackout before the next scene."

"So someone could run on from offstage and make the switch in the dark," Amanda declared.

"Exactly," Dan said.

"But would there be enough time?" Amanda wondered. "The blackout is so short."

"Remember when we timed Kitty yesterday?" Mick countered. "Kitty removed and reloaded that clip in only five seconds."

"That blackout is fifteen," Dan reminded them.

"Hmm." Amanda pursed her lips. "Whoever did it would have to move awfully fast to make the change and get off without running into any actors or furniture."

Mick shrugged. "It's pretty easy if you practice. Dan and I went over it earlier tonight."

"Then what should we do?" Amanda looked from Mick to Dan. "Tell the police?"

Mick shook his head angrily. "Naw, the cops don't care. Dan tried to tell Detective Wick his theory, and he laughed out loud. Said it was impossible. I bet they think this is all a joke."

Dan nodded sadly. "I think he thought I was trying to shift suspicion away from me. The cops are still half-convinced I had something to do with it."

"This is serious," Amanda said. "I mean, Miss Cantwell is doing the show tonight. What's to stop this maniac from trying to get her again?"

"Bingo." Mick pointed a finger at Amanda.

Amanda sat up straight in her chair. "We've got to *do* something!"

"Take it easy," Mick replied with a grin. "Dan and I've come up with a plan." He pulled a piece of paper out of his pocket and smoothed it out on one of the music stands. Dan handed him a penlight. "Here's the layout of the stage. As you can see, there are four ways for someone to get on and off the set." Mick shone the light on the sketch, which showed the two doors and the top of the stairs and the exit that led to the wings.

"Now, if during the performance, Dan and I keep an eye on stage right, and you and Pepper cover stage left, we can nab the person in the blackout and prevent the whole thing."

"But what if the person is one of the actors onstage?" Amanda asked.

"Richard and Miss Cantwell are the only ones out there," Dan replied. "We can figure that Jaqueline didn't do it, and Richard just steps offstage right for a quick change."

"Meanwhile," Mick said, folding up the drawing and tucking it in his pocket, "no one else is supposed to go on in that blackout."

Amanda's throat was dry with fear. She swallowed hard and asked, "What do we do if we see someone?"

Mick rubbed his chin with his hand. "We need a signal. Something to let each other know that we're in trouble."

"How about flashlights?" Dan suggested. "I think we've got enough to go around."

"Perfect." Mick clapped his hands. "At the first hint of anything strange, we flash the light three times on the floor. That'll be the signal for everyone to come help."

"Good," Dan agreed. "And it won't disturb the performance." He checked his watch and stood up. "We'd better get along upstairs."

Mick waved him along. "You go on ahead. I'll be there in a second."

Dan said good-bye and slipped quietly out of the orchestra pit. After he was gone, Mick turned to Amanda. "How do you feel?" he whispered.

"Truthfully?"

Mick nodded.

"Scared silly." Amanda took a deep breath. "So many things could go wrong."

Mick cupped her hand between his. "Nothing will, if you keep your cool, and remember the signal."

"I wish I could be sure about that."

"Hey, trust me. I'll be backstage, and Gabe'll be in the audience. You're covered." Mick turned her hand over, and with one finger he traced a pattern on her palm. "This is your lifeline. It's a long one. I want it to stay that way."

Amanda could feel herself melting at his touch. "You need to be careful, too," she murmured.

"I plan to."

Mick's blue eyes met hers in a steady gaze. He tilted his head slightly, and her heart quickened. Amanda didn't dare breathe. She felt a sudden urge to reach up and tenderly push back the lock of hair that always fell lazily over his eye. Without any effort they seemed to be drawn together. Gently his lips touched hers, and Amanda felt a spark of electricity race through her body. Then a soft noise outside the door stopped them cold.

"Freeze!" Mick whispered.

Amanda held her breath, wondering who might be eavesdropping outside the door. She listened for footsteps, but there were none. Mick carefully reached out his arm and pushed open the door.

"Nobody." He exhaled a sigh of relief.

"Maybe it was one of those theatre ghosts that Teddy's always talking about," Amanda said, trying to sound lighthearted.

"Let's hope so." Mick stepped out into the tunnel, and Amanda followed. For a moment they stood side by side in the darkness. Finally Mick cleared his throat. "I'd better get upstairs. The show is about to start." He turned to leave.

"Mick!" Amanda cried suddenly.

"What?"

A battle of mixed feelings raged inside her. Part of her was still terrified by that breathing they'd heard. Another part of her wished that Mick had ignored the sound and continued with his kiss. She unconsciously touched her mouth where his lips had brushed hers.

"Nothing," Amanda said.

"See you." Mick hurried down the tunnel to the stage.

Amanda started to follow him, then remembered she'd left her apron behind. She stepped back into the orchestra pit. As she did, the little door swung shut behind her.

"Mick?" she called. "Is that you?"

She heard a scraping sound outside the door. Amanda tried to push it open, but it was stuck. "Come on, Mick, is this a joke?"

She tugged at the knob harder. "Because if it is, I'm not laughing."

Amanda pounded on the door and shouted at the top of her lungs, "Mick! Somebody! Get me out of here!"

She paused with her fist in midair as something Teddy had said crept into her brain and froze her blood. *This place is soundproof. People could get trapped down here, scream their lungs out, and no one would ever hear them.*

CHAPTER FIFTEEN

H*elp me!*" Amanda pounded furiously on the door of the orchestra pit. But the thick walls muffled the sound completely. Above her head Amanda could vaguely make out the sound of footsteps onstage. The play had begun, and unless she got out of there soon, a real murder could occur on that stage. She flung herself against the door and beat it with her fists.

No one came. Minutes passed. Amanda pounded on the door for what seemed like hours. Her voice grew hoarse with calling for help.

Finally there was a scraping sound outside the door. Amanda held her breath as the little white door swung open.

"Mr. Verdery!" Amanda gasped as she recognized her rescuer. "What are you doing here?"

"I think I should be asking you that question," he replied. "Don't you realize the second act begins in just a few minutes?"

"I was locked in," Amanda said breathlessly. She clutched at his arm. "Mr. Verdery, you've got to help me. Someone is going to try and murder Miss Cantwell tonight."

His eyes widened with surprise. "Who?"

"I don't know yet," she admitted.

"Is this your high school detective instinct at work again?" he demanded.

Just then Teddy Ballard appeared at the end of the corridor. "Skitch has called places for Act Two, Cliff, and I was wondering if you could go over a line with me— Oh, Amanda, there you are! We were wondering where you'd gone."

"Please, Mr. Verdery, you must listen—"

"I don't have time for your adolescent fantasies right now," the director snapped. "I don't care what the producers say, this is my show and I'm going to make it a success. Now get backstage immediately. I've had my fill of these pranks."

He turned his back and disappeared into the green room with Teddy.

Amanda watched them go, completely frustrated. She hurried up the stairs to the backstage area and was greeted by a distraught Pepper.

"Mandy, where have you been? I've been so worried." Pepper carried two large flashlights, one of which she gave to Amanda.

"Someone locked me in the orchestra pit," Amanda said grimly.

"Oh, my God!" Pepper looked ashen in the dim light.

"Where's Mick?"

"He's with Dan on the other side of the stage."

The lights dimmed for the start of Act Two, and Pepper gulped. "Mandy, I really don't like this. We could get hurt."

"It's too late to stop now," Amanda whispered. "We've got to make sure no one touches that pistol during the blackout."

The curtain rose, and the actors began the second act. Amanda and Pepper quietly took their positions guarding the entrances on their side of the stage. Except for one moment when Pepper had to run off and help with a quick change, their eyes never left the stage.

Amanda gripped her flashlight so tightly that her palms were sweating. Every muscle in her body ached with tension.

As the moment for the blackout neared, Amanda stepped forward behind the library doors. Anyone entering or exiting the set from that point would have to pass by her. Pepper eased herself into the space behind the French doors. Across the stage Amanda could see Mick doing the same thing with the exit on that side.

By the prop table Richard Tyson took the pistol from Dan Carnegie and entered the stage. He set it on the end table, and then he and Jaqueline got into their stage argument that closed the scene. Amanda never took her eyes off the gun, memorizing the exact angle at which it lay on the wooden surface.

The scene ended and the lights went out. Two sets of feet could be heard quietly leaving the stage—the high-heeled click of Jaqueline Cantwell, and the heavier tread of Richard Tyson. Amanda's pulse pounded in her ears as she strained to listen in the dark. She held her breath, waiting for someone to crash into her.

The lights came up again, indicating a new day, and Amanda exhaled. Nothing had changed. The pistol was in the exact same spot as it had been before the lights went out. She was certain of it.

Pepper came up beside her and whispered, "Did you see anything?"

"Nothing," Amanda replied. Across the stage, she caught Mick's eye. He shook his head and shrugged.

"I've got to go help Kitty change," Pepper said, turning to head downstairs. Amanda nodded, but her mind was elsewhere as she frantically tried to figure out what they could have overlooked. Had Dan Carnegie's theory been totally wrong? Or was Dan trying to confuse them? She shook her head in frustration. She needed answers, not more questions. Time was running out.

Then a sound caught her attention. A faint metallic echo rang in her ear. She listened again. Footsteps! And she knew exactly where they were coming from.

Still gripping the flashlight, Amanda stared at the winding metal staircase in the corner. She could barely make out a dark figure slowly climbing toward the prop room. It was too dark to see who it was. She looked over her shoulder to catch Mick's attention. He was leaning over the prop table preparing her tea tray. Carefully she aimed the flashlight at the floor and flashed it three times. He didn't look up.

Great, she thought. *What's the use of a signal if no one sees it?*

Amanda looked back up at the climbing figure. *Maybe it's just Skitch,* she thought, *getting a prop or something.* Then she frowned.

The figure had gone beyond the prop room and was climbing higher into the dark recesses of the stage house. Amanda decided to follow.

By the time she reached the top of the metal staircase, the person was slowly inching out along the catwalk. Rows of lighting instruments hung on either side of the narrow walkway. Amanda carefully stepped out onto the catwalk in pursuit. Her weight shook the metal grating beneath her feet, and the figure gripped the side of the railing to steady himself. In that instant, she recognized him.

He wasn't aware of her. Carefully he reached out to one of the lights and began to loosen the bolt holding the colored gel in front of the lens.

"Alfred!" Amanda hissed. "I wouldn't do that if I were you."

The short, balding man was so startled that he lost his balance and nearly fell backward off the catwalk. Amanda gripped the railing as the catwalk started to shake.

"I wasn't d-doing anything," he stammered.

"I saw you tampering with that light."

"But I was just going to drop the gel." His face tensed. "Not on anyone, mind you, but just onto the floor. To scare the audience."

"Why?"

His face started to twitch. "To sell more tickets. The accidents are the only reason they're coming to see my play."

Amanda couldn't help feeling sorry for the pathetic little man. "Is that why you tried to rig the wall to fall?"

He nodded sadly and stared down at his feet. "But I had nothing to do with all those other awful accidents. Please believe me."

He acted like a little boy caught with his hand in the cookie jar, not like a cold-blooded murderer planning his second attempt.

"I think you should go back downstairs and watch the play from the audience," Amanda said firmly. "You'd be surprised, it might just be good enough to run on its own, without all of these publicity stunts."

"Do you think so?"

Amanda nodded, then looked pointedly toward the stairs. As she watched him inch his way back to the metal staircase and slowly descend the steps, she made a mental note to talk to Detective Wick about Alfred's confession. Amanda glanced down from her perch and suddenly realized she could see everything that was happening on and off the stage. She watched Alfred leave the circular staircase and disappear into the darkness.

Onstage, Jaqueline Cantwell was making a dramatic farewell speech and seemed to glow with energy. The only sign that she'd had a near brush with death was the small white bandage wrapped around her wrist.

Off in the wings, Skitch, her headset firmly on top of her head, busily called each cue from a huge notebook sitting next to the control board. Every now and then she would look at the stage, and then one of the lights near Amanda would change in intensity.

Further off, Pepper and the ladies from wardrobe were busy holding clothes for Kitty, who was about to change into her dress for the big apparition scene.

Mick stood by the prop table. He had changed into a black turtleneck sweater, and in the half-light, Amanda thought he looked more like a movie star than any of the men on the stage. She felt butterflies in her stomach as she remembered the moment when they kissed.

I'd better be getting downstairs myself, she thought. Her entrance was coming up, and as far as she could tell, Cliff Verdery hadn't appeared yet to help her make it onto the stage. Amanda took one last glance at Mick before heading down.

Suddenly a large hand grabbed her from behind and yanked her head back roughly. A piece of cloth was stuffed in her mouth, and a long piece of silver duct tape pressed across her lips.

She fought back, but her assailant pulled her arms behind her and wrenched them up sharply. The searing pain took her breath away. He forced her to her knees on the narrow catwalk. The metal grating dug into her skin and she wanted to cry out, but the gag choked her. Holding her arms tightly, her attacker bound them with duct tape around the railing. The tape made a horrible ripping sound as he wound the roll around and around her wrists.

Amanda tried to twist her head to identify her attacker, but her face was wedged between two brightly burning lights. Their intense heat was almost unbearable. The stage swirled beneath her in a blur, and she thought she would faint.

Then a voice snarled in her ear, "I'll deal with you later."

CHAPTER SIXTEEN

Amanda was helpless. Her shoulders and hands were growing numb, and the metal grate dug painfully into her knees. Her head throbbed as she watched the action on the stage. Who had done this to her?

Please, Mick, she pleaded soundlessly, *see that I'm not there.* Below her, Teddy Ballard entered and was speaking with Kitty on the stage. Amanda watched the actor open his cigarette case and pull out a long white cigarette.

My entrance! she thought. *I'm going to miss my entrance!*

Colonel Pinchmore would stop by the desk, light the cigarette, and then move up to the French doors. That was when she was to enter with the tea.

Amanda shifted her head and accidentally bumped the hot lamp beside her. The light thrown onto the set bounced with the movement. Amanda looked down hopefully at the actors to see if anyone had noticed and gasped at what she saw. In a flash she knew how the switch had been done.

Of course! her mind screamed. *Dan was right. The clip gets switched onstage. And it happens in full view of the audience!*

She tried frantically to pull the tape off her wrists. Each passing second was a missed chance to save a life. Her head banged the light again, and this time it flickered on and off. Mick's words ran through her brain. *If you're in trouble, flash three times.*

Amanda squeezed her eyes tight and hit the light with all her might. The lamp's edge caught her just above the ear. She bumped it again, managing to depress the shutter lever. A shadow crossed the stage. Amanda craned her eyes to the right. She could see that Skitch had noticed something was wrong. Amanda hit the switch again, and again. This time, Skitch glanced up at the catwalk. Her mouth dropped open when she saw Amanda.

"Tea would be lovely just about now, don't you think so, Colonel Pinchmore?" Kitty was saying onstage. "I wonder where Dora is."

It was Amanda's missed entrance, and Kitty was trying to cover for her. "Dora? Is that you?" Kitty peered offstage. There was an awkward silence, and she giggled shrilly. "I guess it was just my imagination." She raised her voice and glared into the wings. "I was *certain* it was tea time."

Meanwhile, Amanda saw that Skitch had deserted the console. Looking toward the staircase, she saw the stage manager and another person clambering up to help her.

Hurry! Amanda urged them silently. In a few moments, Kitty would pick up the pistol and pull the trigger, and Jaqueline . . . The words of Maggie's threatening note echoed through her brain: *"Next time the bullet won't miss!"* She struggled even harder to free her wrists. Sweat poured down her face from the fierce heat of the lights.

"Did someone call for me?" a familiar voice sounded on the stage. Amanda peered down on the set, and nearly choked. Pepper was standing center stage, clutching the tea tray, staring out at the audience. Her maid's uniform consisted of an old print apron tied around her jeans. A bandana was pinned clumsily to her curly red hair. If things hadn't been so awful, Amanda would have laughed.

"Dora! I'm so glad you're here!" Kitty rushed to Pepper's side and snatched the tray out of her hands. "The colonel and I were *dying* for a cup of tea."

Kitty's final words prompted Pepper to remember Amanda's one line. "Tea is served—I mean, here is your tea, miss."

Kitty's eyes widened, but she replied calmly, "Thank you, Dora."

Pepper remained frozen in the center of the stage. Amanda realized that her friend's stage fright was buying time. *Just keep it up, Pepper,* she begged sound-lessly, *do anything until Skitch gets here.*

"I said, thank you, Pepper—I mean, Dora." Kitty was getting flustered. "Now, please stand over there by the sideboard."

Pepper walked stiffly to the sideboard and asked, "Here?"

Several people in the audience snickered, and Pepper squinted out in the direction of the giggling, which prompted some more people to laugh out loud.

"And stay there until I need you!" Kitty shouted at Pepper.

Pepper held up her palms and muttered, "Okay, okay." She leaned up against the sideboard with her arms folded across her chest. Now the audience was howling.

Amanda felt the catwalk shudder with the weight of running feet. Help was finally at hand.

Onstage, Kitty resolutely went on with the play. "Tea is served, Colonel Pinchmore." She tapped him on the shoulder. "Colonel? Are you ill?"

Teddy spun around, clutching the bloody knife stuck into his chest. There was a gasp from the audience as he staggered for the desk. Hearing their response made him prolong his death agonies even more than usual. Finally, with a horrific shudder, he collapsed across the sofa.

Richard Tyson dashed in through the stage-left door and cried, "How could you?"

Then Amanda felt strong hands pull her up from the metal grate.

"This will hurt only for a second," Skitch's voice murmured in her ear. There was a sharp tug, a fierce pain as the tape was ripped off her mouth, and then cool air poured into her lungs. Cliff Verdery was kneeling beside the stage manager. Using a penknife, he hurriedly cut the tape away from her wrists. Amanda glanced down at the stage and saw Kitty pick up the pistol.

"Stop the play," she rasped hoarsely. "That gun is loaded!"

The stage manager's eyes grew huge with horror. She turned and raced back down the catwalk. Cliff Verdery snipped the last strip of tape away and helped Amanda to her feet.

The world spun crazily around her. She clutched at the railing, desperately trying to get the wooziness out of her stomach and head. Onstage Kitty shouted, "Stay away from me, all of you!" Thick white wisps of fog poured over the top of the casement stairs, signaling Jaqueline's entrance. Taking a deep breath, Amanda made her way as fast as she could off the catwalk, with the director right behind her. The two of them clattered down the metal staircase.

The casement windows swung open, and the apparition appeared at the top of the stairs. "Eloise," it intoned eerily, "you must pay for your sins!"

Kitty turned and aimed the pistol at the swirling image. At the same moment, Skitch screamed, "Kitty, don't shoot!"

The cry startled her, and Kitty jerked her hand

back. The pistol went off, and a bullet ripped a hole in the wall of the set. Kitty shrieked and dropped the gun. Then Amanda raced onto the stage and shouted, "Teddy Ballard is the murderer!"

CHAPTER SEVENTEEN

Teddy Ballard, who was sprawled across the sofa with a knife sticking out of his chest, sat up, and the audience gasped. They thought Colonel Pinchmore had come back to life.

Everyone stood frozen, unsure of what to do. Teddy calmly rose to his feet, a slow smile covering his lips.

"An interesting twist, Miss Hart," he drawled. One hand slipped into his coat pocket and Amanda tensed. She'd seen him make the same move only moments before from the catwalk.

"Well, now, there's been no murder, has there?" Teddy said in his suavest voice, all the while inching toward center stage. "At least, not yet." His eyes darted toward the pistol lying at Kitty's feet.

"I wouldn't do that if I were you," the apparition

warned from the top of the steps. Teddy looked up in surprise, then dove for the pistol. The white figure leaped all the way to the floor and tackled Teddy. Then it ripped the knife off his chest, flipped the actor onto his stomach, and pinned his hands behind him.

"Teddy, I don't believe it."

Everyone gasped as Jaqueline Cantwell stepped into a pool of light by the side of the stage.

"Jaqui?" Teddy turned his head from Jaqueline to the masked figure, and back again. "It can't be . . ."

Amanda was equally confused. If Jaqueline was standing in front of them, then who was wearing her white costume?

In one swift movement the apparition ripped off the mask and wig.

"Mick!" Amanda gasped as he picked up the pistol and trained it on Teddy. The actor slowly got to his feet.

"Just hold it right there," Mick said quietly. "And don't make any sudden movements."

Jaqueline moved center stage and said in a near whisper, "I don't understand. Why? You were my dearest friend."

"Ha!" Teddy sneered. "I am your bitterest enemy. I loved you, and you killed that love."

"Oh, Teddy—"

"Thirty years ago you broke my heart, but did you give a damn? All that mattered to you was your career. You married George and used him, just as you've used every person you've ever known."

"That's a lie!"

Teddy Ballard's eyes were glazed, and he spoke as if he were in a trance. "But I loved you—so I waited. I waited for you to reach your dream of success. I was sure you'd drop George and return to me because, deep down, I knew you loved me, not him."

"Teddy, this is too much." Jaqueline turned her head away.

"And why shouldn't I have thought that? Whenever you had problems, who did you turn to? Good old Teddy. 'Teddy will understand—I can pour my heart out to Teddy.'"

"You were my good friend," Jaqueline whispered. "That's all."

Teddy didn't seem to hear. His voice grew stronger as he spoke. "When George died, I thought, 'Now it's my turn.'" His shoulders began to shake. "But you shut me out. You walked away from the theatre and for ten lonely years, you never gave me a second thought."

"But, Teddy, that's not true," Jaqueline protested. "I gave you a part in my play."

"A bit part!" he shouted. "One more bone thrown to your devoted dog." He struggled to control himself. "My entire life spent waiting for *you*." Teddy lowered his voice, his face contorted with hatred. "Thirty years ago you murdered me. Now I'm going to murder you—if it's the last thing I do!"

Thinking the actor was going to attack Jaqueline Cantwell, Mick jumped in front to protect her. But Teddy ran for the edge of the stage and leaped into the audience. As he bolted up the center aisle, a husky figure in black stepped out and blocked his escape.

"Get him, Gabe!" Mick shouted.

Within seconds Gabe had wrestled him to the ground. A swarm of ushers and security guards came to help hustle him into the lobby.

From the stage, Jaqueline Cantwell pointed a finger at Teddy and commanded, "Take him away—the traitor!"

The audience, who had been mesmerized by the scene, suddenly burst into loud applause. Everyone onstage turned to face them in surprise. They'd forgotten anyone was there.

"What do we do?" Amanda hissed out of the corner of her mouth.

"For heaven's sake, pull the curtain!" The order came from Jaqueline, who'd somehow managed to speak without moving her lips as she leaned tragically against the wall of the set. Skitch dashed into the wings, and moments later the red curtain came down in front of them. Meanwhile, the audience cheered enthusiastically.

As soon as the curtain had shut, Amanda ran to Mick. "Are you okay? I couldn't believe it was you in that costume."

"When you didn't appear onstage, I knew something was up. I alerted Dan, and we agreed that I should go on for Jaqui."

"But that was very dangerous."

"Naw." Mick grinned as he pulled open the front of

the white gown. He had strapped a brass shield from the prop room across his chest. He removed it and tapped it with his hand. "This thing will stop a grenade!"

Pepper, her eyes wide with shock, joined them. "That was the scariest moment of my entire life!"

"You mean, when Teddy grabbed for the gun?" Amanda asked.

"No, when I had to walk out onstage in front of all those people—and talk!"

"Listen to that applause!" Alfred Crane said, rushing in from the wings. His face was flushed with excitement. "We're a hit!"

Kitty hugged Amanda. "I knew you'd figure this out."

Amanda's knees suddenly felt a little wobbly as she remembered what she had just gone through.

"How did you ever guess that it was Teddy?" Mick asked, slipping an arm around her waist.

Amanda pointed up into the rafters of the theatre. "I saw him make the switch from the catwalk."

Mick's eyes widened. "What were you doing up there?"

"I'll tell you all about it later," Amanda replied with a tired smile.

"But how'd Teddy do it?" Pepper asked. "I mean, I was right there next to him the whole time."

Amanda chuckled. "You were there, all right, but from what I could see, you looked almost catatonic. I doubt if you would have noticed anything."

"What do you expect?" Pepper grumbled. "I didn't even have a costume."

"But I was there, too," Kitty interrupted, "and I didn't see him do it. How'd he manage it?"

"Remember when Teddy walked up to the desk and lit the cigarette?"

"Who could forget?" Mick said. "He does that neat little flourish with the lighter in his left hand. Really grabs your attention."

"I get it," Richard Tyson said, coming up to join them. "While he drew our focus with one hand, he was palming the pistol with the other."

Amanda nodded. "Exactly. Then, while the audience thought he was smoking a cigarette at the French doors, and we all thought he was attaching that prop knife to his chest, he was really changing the clip, exchanging the blanks for live bullets."

"But how did he put it back?" Pepper asked.

"Same thing," Amanda said. "During his big death scene Teddy paused at the desk to make some gruesome faces—"

"And that's when he dropped the gun back on the desk!" Pepper exclaimed.

"Just in time for Kitty to grab it."

"Wow!" Kitty shook her head in amazement. "I thought Teddy was just an old ham, when he was really sort of a clever magician."

"And a good con man," Mick added. "He would have played us all for suckers if Mandy hadn't caught his act."

Behind the curtain they could hear the audience clapping in unison. Alfred squealed, "They're going crazy out there. Somebody take a bow!"

Cliff Verdery shook his head. "I don't get it. The play's not over yet."

"Yes, it is," Alfred breathed. "And this ending is terrific. Much better than the one George—I mean, I wrote."

Jaqueline, who had been standing quietly by the side of the stage, suddenly came to life. "Alfred's right. The ending has always lacked something. I think this is just what the play needs—that extra element of surprise."

"But that would mean some rewriting," Cliff said.

"I'm willing," Alfred said. "After all, I've waited this long for my play to open. I might as well make sure it's a success."

Cliff scratched his chin. "You know, I have a few ideas about how to integrate the new ending with the first act."

"Great!" Alfred said. "I can use the help." He turned to Jaqueline. "That is, if you don't mind Cliff's coming back to the show."

"Of course not, darling," Jaqueline flashed a brilliant smile. "I don't mind anything that will make this show a hit."

"Great!" Cliff draped one arm over Alfred's shoulder. "The part I thought worked the best was when he"—the director pointed at Mick—"came on disguised as Jaqueline."

Jaqueline raised an eyebrow at Mick. "Yes, it seems

you are quite the master of disguises, Mr. Michael
. . . um, what was your last name?"

Mick could only stammer as he realized Jaqueline
had recognized him from the hospital. He turned to
Amanda for help.

The applause surged, and Skitch shouted, "I'm
opening the curtain. Line up, everybody."

The next thing she knew, Amanda was standing with
Mick and the rest of the cast in front of two thousand
people, who were on their feet cheering.

One by one each actor stepped forward to take a
bow. Even Pepper trotted to center stage and curtsied
awkwardly. She raced back to join the lineup and
shoved Mick and Amanda hard. "Your turn!"

The two of them stumbled forward, and the applause swelled for the mystery couple who had appeared at the end of the play.

Mick bowed first to Amanda and then out to the
audience. Amanda managed a quick nod. Then, in a
move that surprised everyone—but no one more than
Amanda—Mick took Amanda by the hand and twirled
her into his arms. The audience roared its approval.

Mick looked into her green eyes and whispered,
"Listen to that applause. That's from the audience.
And this"—he bent down and placed his lips against
hers—"is from me."

Mick's arms tightened around her, and Amanda
could feel the tingle of his kiss down to her toes.

Suddenly she didn't care that two thousand people
were watching. Amanda wrapped her arms around

Mick's neck and kissed him back. She had waited months for this moment, and it was worth it.

Cheers of "Bravo!" echoed throughout the theatre. But no one cheered louder than Pepper Larson, who knew that Hart and Soul belonged together.

ABOUT THE AUTHOR

JAHNNA N. MALCOLM is really the pen name for a husband and wife team, Jahnna Beecham and Malcolm Hillgartner. Together they have written twenty-one books, including five titles for Bantam's Sweet Dreams series under the name Jahnna Beecham. They are also the authors of a middle-grade series called Bad News Ballet. Both are professional actors and have trod the boards in theatres across the United States and Europe. In fact, they met in an audition and were married on the stage. Jahnna and Malcolm live in Montana with their brand-new baby Dashiell and two old dogs.

We hope you enjoyed reading this book. If you would like to receive further information about available titles in the Bantam series, just write to the address below, with your name and address: Kim Prior, Bantam Books, 61–63 Uxbridge Road, Ealing, London W5 5SA.

If you live in Australia or New Zealand and would like more information about the series, please write to:

Sally Porter
Transworld Publishers
(Australia) Pty Ltd
15-23 Helles Avenue
Moorebank
NSW 2170
AUSTRALIA

Kiri Martin
Transworld Publishers (NZ) Ltd
Cnr. Moselle and Waipareira
Avenues
Henderson
Auckland
NEW ZEALAND

All Bantam and Young Adult books are available at your bookshop or newsagent, or can be ordered at the following address: Corgi/Bantam Books, Cash Sales Department, PO Box 11, Falmouth, Cornwall, TR10 9EN.

Please list the title(s) you would like, and send together with a cheque or postal order. You should allow for the cost of book(s) plus postage and packing charges as follows:

80p for one book
£1.00 for two books
£1.20 for three books
£1.40 for four books
Five or more books free.

Please note that payment must be made in pounds sterling; other currencies are unacceptable.

(The above applies to readers in the UK and Republic of Ireland only)

BFPO customers, please allow for the cost of the book(s) plus the following for postage and packing: 80p for the first book, and 20p for each additional copy.

Overseas customers, please allow £1.50 for postage and packing for the first book, £1.00 for the second book, and 30p for each subsequent title ordered.

SWEET VALLEY HIGH

The top-selling teenage series starring identical twins Jessica and Elizabeth Wakefield and all their friends at Sweet Valley High. One new title every month!

1. DOUBLE LOVE
2. SECRETS
3. PLAYING WITH FIRE
4. POWER PLAY
5. ALL NIGHT LONG
6. DANGEROUS LOVE
7. DEAR SISTER
8. HEARTBREAKER
9. RACING HEARTS
10. WRONG KIND OF GIRL
11. TOO GOOD TO BE TRUE
12. WHEN LOVE DIES
21. RUNAWAY
25. NOWHERE TO RUN
28. ALONE IN THE CROWD
33. STARTING OVER
40. ON THE EDGE
44. PRETENCES

49. PLAYING FOR KEEPS
51. AGAINST THE ODDS
54. TWO-BOY WEEKEND
55. PERFECT SHOT
60. THAT FATAL NIGHT
61. BOY TROUBLE
62. WHO'S WHO?
63. THE NEW ELIZABETH
67. THE PARENT PLOT
68. THE LOVE BET
69. FRIEND AGAINST FRIEND
70. MS QUARTERBACK
71. STARRING JESSICA
72. ROCK STAR'S GIRL
73. REGINA'S LEGACY
74. THE PERFECT GIRL
75. AMY'S TRUE LOVE

SWEET VALLEY SUPER STARS

1. LILA'S STORY
2. BRUCE'S STORY
3. ENID'S STORY

PEN PALS

by Sharon Dennis Wyeth

How do four boy-crazy girls meet four girl-crazy boys? They place an ad for PEN PALS, of course! Well, that's what Lisa, Shanon, Amy and Palmer (otherwise known as the Foxes) do – and it's not long before they get a reply! An irresistibly entertaining new series.